TEARS OF JOY
AN UNTOLD STORY OF TWO ANGELS

by

Joseph Tristan

DORRANCE
PUBLISHING CO
EST. 1920
PITTSBURGH, PENNSYLVANIA 15238

Dorrance Publishing Co
585 Alpha Drive
Pittsburgh, PA 15238
Visit our website at *www.dorrancebookstore.com*

ISBN: 978-1-6495-7269-1
eISBN: 978-1-6495-7773-3

DEDICATION

This story is dedicated to the Angels that live among us
and
To the Angels that were called home before our
hearts could say goodbye.

Joseph Tristan

Bonus: "True Love" by Joseph Tristan

A note from Joseph Tristan:

Tears of Joy: An Untold Story of Two Angels is a story of fiction; however, the first two parts of the story "No One Fights Alone" and "A New Journey Begins" telling of Cathy's battle to defeat a vicious, unforgiving monster are based on true events. The story features a publication titled *Cathy's Corner* that was sent to her support team regularly.

I have included *Cathy's Corner* in my story in its original content, except for photos that were featured in some of the publications due to privacy rights. I did include pictures of Cathy and her family in certain publications.

My intent in including the publications was to have my readers feel that they are a member of "Cathy's Corner" as well.

A special "Thank you" to Ms. Kellie for providing missing publications of Cathy's Corner from her archives.

I trust you will enjoy reading "Tears of Joy" as much as I did writing it.

Feel free to reach out to me with your thoughts or comments at joseph.tristan953@gmail.com

PROLOGUE

The call of mother nature awakened Cathy. As she looked over at her alarm clock, she quietly moaned to herself, "It is too early for me to be getting out of this comfortable bed, but it looks like I don't have any other option." She removed herself from her warm bed and slowly proceeded to the bathroom to take care of her business. A few minutes later, she walked gingerly to the kitchen to turn on the stove to heat the pot of water that would soon be poured into her french press coffee glass container. Five minutes later, she would have an outstanding cup of fresh coffee. Cathy always started her day with a first-rate cup of coffee that gave her the vitality to get her body to wake up. If not physically at least mentally.

Cathy sat down at the kitchen table and thought, after this cup of coffee, she was going to make herself a hearty breakfast of bacon and eggs. For the time being, she was going to sit at the table, enjoying her first cup of coffee of the day. As she was sitting there, she started to replay the previous evening's celebration of her eighty-fifth birthday. She sat there and thought to herself, *I can't believe that I am eighty-five years old; it seems like yesterday I was sixty-five.* Cathy started to laugh out loud when she recalled telling people that she was sixty-five years old, then with a smile, she would say twenty years ago. The real humor was watching a person's face as they stood there trying to add sixty-five plus twenty.

While Cathy sat on her chair with circling thoughts of her life going through her mind, she was interrupted by the voice of her granddaughter Addison as she closed the front door, yelling, "GiGi, I am here, where are you?"

Cathy smiled as she replied, "I am in the kitchen enjoying my coffee." She added, "Gosh, girl, do you have to yell so loud; you will wake up the dead."

Addison laughed as she bent down to give GiGi a morning kiss and said, "I yell that loud just in case you fall asleep and decide to never wake up without telling me goodbye."

Addison sat down at the table and told Cathy that she decided to come over and spend the morning with her to help get the house back to "Gigi's level of clean." Addison went to the stove to get herself a fresh cup of coffee and returned to the table. "So tell me, did you enjoy your birthday party last night?" asked Addison.

Cathy smiled back, saying, "Yes, it was very nice, and I appreciate everything you and the family did to make it a fabulous night for me."

Addison had a worried look on her face as she looked into Cathy's eyes and said, "Before we start cleaning, can I talk to you about something that is on my mind?"

"Of course, Addison, you know that you can always talk to me. Now tell me what is on my favorite granddaughters mind?" replied Cathy.

Addison laughed, "Gigi, I am your favorite granddaughter because you only have one granddaughter, *me.*

Cathy laughed in return as she said, "That definitely puts the odds in your favor. Now please tell me what is on your mind."

Addison started telling Cathy, "Last night, as I was walking around thanking the guests for coming, we started to talk about you, your life, and celebrating your eighty-five birthday. During more than one of the conversations, a guest would comment on how great it was that you are still with us after your sickness some years back that almost took your life. I was surprised to hear the comments because I was unaware of a sickness that almost killed you. Gigi, did you almost die?"

Without hesitating, Cathy looked at Addison with tears in her eyes and answered, "Yes, honey, death was on my doorstep. I thought that I was going to die as it was a very serious sickness and I was not sure it could be stopped."

Addison quickly replied, "I had no idea, you and Papa Joe never talked about your sickness or how you got well. Why did you not tell my brother, Christan, or me about you being sick?"

Cathy sat back in her chair and stated, "Addison it was a long time ago, back around 2013, it was a two-year battle, and when it was over, your grandpa, and I never spoke of it. We moved forward in our life together, enjoying every day we had doing things that made us happy, like watching you and your brother grow up to be the beautiful young adults that you are."

"But Gigi," Addison cried out, "I love you very much, and I feel bad that you were sick, and I was not there to help."

Cathy touched Addison's hand and smiled. "Listen, my Georgia Peach, it was a long time ago, and you were just born the year I got sick. The day you were born, Papa Joe and I drove to Georgia from our home in Florida to see the first girl born in our family. Papa Joe and I raised three boys, and your brother, Christan, was born first in your family. We were anxiously waiting for the first girl to join our family tree.

"It was two weeks after we returned to Florida from our visit with you. I went into the hospital to see what was wrong with my body."

Addison sat back folded her arms as she exclaimed, "Okay, I understand the part of me being young, but I am now twenty-eight years old; you never told me about being sick. So, the doctors and nurses found out what was wrong and treated you to good health?"

Cathy looked back at Addison as she revealed to her, "Yes, the doctors and nurses did everything they could do, but to be honest with you, Addison, I was saved by an Angel."

Addison's eyes grew the size of a fifty-cent coin as she shouted, "An angel, a real living angel? You have to be kidding me. Gigi, this I have to hear, a real angel? Okay, let's put the house cleaning on hold. Please tell me everything about your sickness and how an angel saved you."

Cathy just sat there as she calmly replied, "Before we have any discussion about my sickness, go into my bedroom, and in the bottom drawer of my nightstand there is a book; please go and bring it to me."

Addison quickly jumped from the table and ran into the bedroom. Cathy could hear her open the drawer and mumble, "Okay, book, where are you? Gigi said you were in here." After moving a few articles of clothing, Addison found the book Cathy was referring to. She quickly looked at the book cover and gasped when she read the title: *"Tears of Joy," An Untold Story of Two Angels* by Joseph Tristan.

Addison ran back to the kitchen, clutching the book in her hand. She cried out to Cathy, "Here it is, I found it. But why did you want me to bring it to you."

Cathy answered, "The beginning of this story is based on the true events of my fight to beat a horrible monster. I think that Joseph Tristan tells my story better than I can remember at my age.

Why don't you and I sit on the couch as you read the story? That way I can answer any questions you may have."

Addison went to the stove, refilled her coffee cup, took Cathy's hand, and together they walked into the family room and sat on the couch. Addison once again looked at the cover of the book and asked Cathy, "Joseph Tristan... that name sounds familiar. Where have I heard the name before?"

Cathy laughed and uttered, "Let's read the book first, and when you are done, I will tell you about Joseph Tristan."

"NO ONE FIGHTS ALONE"

1.

It was July 3, the day before the Fourth of July, America's birthday, which meant that the day would be filled with the never-ending preparations for the annual neighborhood cookout at Cathy's house. It was a special time where friends and neighbors gathered to eat excellent food, like her husband Joe's, smoked potato salad, which the neighbors would say that was the real reason they came every year. The time was spent drinking a few brews, sharing the past year's happenings, and, most importantly, time laughing with the people that brought happiness and pleasure to the neighborhood.

However, those plans quickly evaporated to distant thoughts that would not return for at least two years once that fateful phone call on the morning of July 3.

Cathy knew that there was something wrong; she was always tired and kept getting black and blue marks all over her body. It seemed that all you had to do was touch her and her skin would become a dark black and blue, resembling the same effect as if she was beaten with a baseball bat. She had recently gone to her doctor the prior week, where they drew blood and said that they would run some tests to see what was going on with her body. They said that they should know something in about six or seven days.

When the July 3 phone call came, little did Cathy realize that it would be the call that would change her life forever. A call that would soon bring to life, a person's greatest fears, greatest challenges, and greatest joys. It would be a two-year roller coaster ride that would have moments of great highs and tremendous lows as her fight to live would take every bit of energy that she, her husband, family, and friends, had to beat the unknown monster they were about to face head-on.

The doctor did not say what was wrong, but rather she needed to stop what she was doing and go to the emergency room. Her doctor explained that she would phone the hospital and explain that she was on her way. Fear and panic went through her body like a lightning bolt, and her eyes filled with tears

Cathy immediately went to her job's H.R. manager's office to inform her that she had to leave and that she did not know when she would be back, tears flowing down her face like a small creek. On her way to the hospital, she phoned Joe. She brought him up to date on what transpired. He told her he was on his way and would meet her at the hospital.

After her husband arrived, they were placed in the observation room as they were waiting for a room to become available. Their minds went wild trying to figure out what could be wrong, but no definitive conclusion could be made. The nurses came in two additional times to draw more blood samples. The hospital admissions clerk came to the room and told her how sorry she was for her being sick and that they were doing everything to find a room to help make her well again. However, the clerk mentioned that when they were checking with her primary medical carrier, as they were told that Cathy still had $1,700 remaining on her deductible balance, and how did she want to take care of this deductible balance charge. After giving the clerk her credit card and satisfying the hospital's endless worry about how they were going to be paid, Cathy was thanked and told to get well soon.

After five to six hours of waiting in the observation room, Cathy was told that they had a place for her, and she was going to be transported to her new room. When she asked about the results of her blood tests, she was notified that the results were not back yet, and they would let her know as soon as they had the results.

As Cathy and her spouse came off the third-floor elevator as she was being transported to her room, it did not take them long to see that they were on the Oncology floor, and their first thought was, *is this a temporary stop or a permanent stay?* They will learn that answer in the morning, but for now, the best thing they could do was try to get some sleep after a long and stressful day.

As Joe was driving home, he spent most of his drive trying to find the words for what was happening. He called his three sons and explained that Cathy was in the hospital. He updated them on everything that had transpired since Cathy was admitted earlier that afternoon. Joe stated that he would keep them updated as soon as he received any new information.

Unfortunately, the phone calls to their sons did not bring any relief of the day's events. His emotions were like a roller coaster ride, and he struggled to tell the boys not to worry, for he was sure that whatever the problem is, there will be medicine to help.

Little did he know that he was in for the longest roller coaster ride of his life. As Joe finished his calls, he noticed flashes of light in the dark sky ahead of his car. He then realized that many of the communities were doing their July 4th fireworks on July 3rd, this would enable everyone to have a fun start to a long three-day weekend. It took only seconds before Joe's mind blanked out the outside activities as he mentally retreated back to his circling thoughts.

His greatest fear was how his wife would handle the situation if it were severe. He always looked for the silver lining, and his wife would initially look at the downside until he could point out the silver lining or help her see the positive side of things. Joe knew that whatever the diagnosis would turn out to be, he needed to be prepared to develop a plan of action that would get Cathy well regardless of the time and expense. The only thing he could do at present was getting a good night's sleep, which probably would not happen, and wait for the results from the blood work to explain what was happening to his wife. Hopefully, tomorrow would be a day of good news.

2.

The next morning had dawned, and Cathy woke up waiting for Joe to arrive and the results of the blood tests. The world outside the hospital room was filled with Fourth of July festivities with plans of cookouts and fireworks. Cathy realized that this Fourth of July would be different for her. Besides, finding out was wrong with her, and getting well was her top priority right now in life.

However, little did she know at the time the answer she was waiting for would put on hold any plans of family or holiday celebrations for at least three years.

It did not take long for the nurses to come in and inform Cathy that with the holiday, it would take a day or two longer get all the results and have the doctor analyze them before telling her what the final diagnosis was. Needless to say, the news sunk their heart into their stomachs, knowing they would have to continue to wait. The only relief they felt was knowing they would finally get a definite answer rather than playing the guessing game of Cathy's diagnosis.

The next morning Cathy phoned Joe and said to him that the P.A. for the oncology floor had stopped in her room to introduce herself and announce that her doctor was going to be Dr. Lukeman for the time being. She also informed Cathy that Dr. Lukeman would be in on Sunday at 8:00 a.m. to discuss all the results from the blood tests and what course of action was on the list. So, the wait continued for the time being; however, the P.A. did stop in and tell Cathy that one of the tests showed that her platelet level was deficient and a possible contributing factor to her illness. She stated that normal platelet levels should be between 250-400 (thousand), and hers came in at 14 (thousand), so the first course of action was to get the platelet level to a more normal level. As bad as this sounded, Cathy felt a little relieved because her oldest son had had a problem with his platelets and had to go through some tough steroids and drugs to get his body to increase its production of platelets. She thought, *Okay, at least it is something that medication can resolve,* and she started to breathe a little easier. As she lay back and took a deep breath, her nose began to bleed at which she said, "Great, now my nose is bleeding. What is next?" As her husband looked on, this was the moment he knew what was wrong but also knew to keep it to himself for the time being, at least until Sunday morning at 8:00 where Cathy would experience a kind of fear she never knew she would or could experience.

Sunday at 8:00 a.m., Dr. Lukeman came into Cathy's hospital room, where both Cathy and Joe were anxiously waiting to hear what was happening. It took her only a few sentences to deliver the news. She stated the results are back, and I have confirmed that you have ALL-T-cell (Acute Lymphocytic Leukemia.)

> *(Acute lymphocytic Leukemia (ALL) is a cancer of the blood and bone marrow. In ALL, there's an increase in a type of white blood cell (WBC) known as a lymphocyte. Because it's an acute, or aggressive, form of cancer, it moves rapidly. ALL is the most common childhood cancer. Children younger than age 5 have the highest risk. It can also occur in adults when they get into their fifties.*

There are two main subtypes of ALL, B-cell ALL and T-cell ALL. Most types of ALL can be treated with a good chance of remission in children. However, adults with ALL don't have as high of a remission rate, but it's steadily improving.) nm, The National Cancer Institute (NCI) estimates 5,960 people in the United States will receive a diagnosis of ALL each year.)

To date, the cause of ALL T-Cell is still unknown to today's medical science teams.

Dr. Lukeman continued to inform Cathy and Joe, "This is a cancer of the blood, and you are in the late stage of this cancer." She stated that she felt that this was the case from your earlier tests, "but I needed the bone marrow test results to come back to confirm my suspicions." She continued, "Now, if you are going to get cancer, this is one that you would want to get, not that there is good cancer but because this one is very treatable and has a fairly good success rate of survival in children."

Dr. Lukeman explained that this leukemia was not a result of a lifestyle situation. That the medical research teams have yet to determine the cause of this leukemia other than it is a cancer of the blood. Dr. Lukeman continued to say that there was no guarantee that she will be able to achieve remission with this leukemia. Still, she has the knowledge and type of chemo treatments to give it a counterpunch that could give Cathy a fighting chance to win this upcoming fight. Dr. Lukeman explained that the treatment would begin that day, and she would be in the hospital for at least another week or so receiving continuous chemo treatment the whole time.

She explained that it would be an eight-month cycle of ongoing chemo treatment that would involve two different levels of chemo, one will be a very aggressive treatment that will last two weeks with the second treatment cycle being a lesser aggressive type of chemo with another two-week time period. The treatment cycle will alternate with each hospital stay. There will also be six spinal tap treatments, "where my medical team will insert a large needle in your spine to extract spinal fluids from the spine." This was a necessary procedure to make sure that cancer has not entered the spinal fluids, for if it did, it would eventually flow up to the brain.

Cathy and Joe were then told that a nurse would be in shortly to explain the treatment process and the numerous side effects of the chemo treatment as it was killing the blood cells in her body. The consultation took over two hours as the nurse covered all of the treatments, the possible side effects, and potential dangers of chemotherapy, such as destroying her organs as well as cancer. When the consultation had ended, it was apparent by the look on Cathy's face and the fear in her eyes. Cathy was truly scared. Not only did she have leukemia that was going to kill if not treated, but she was also going to have a chemo treatment program that was extremely aggressive. The chemo treatment side effects in itself could cause severe damage to her internal organs and cause her death. Cathy closed her eyes as a stream of tears were flowing down the side of her face.

The fear of what was happening was stressing her to a level that she has never experienced. She would lay there and think, *this cannot be happening to me, I feel that I am in a no-win situation. If I don't start chemo, I am going to die; if I start chemo, the side effects could be so severe I could die.* After a few minutes, Cathy took a deep breath and said to herself, *Okay, Lord, it is up to you and me (with the help of Joe) to beat this ugly monster. I have to tell you Lord I have never been so scared in my life as I am now, but I am going to fight this monster with everything I have. So, you and Joe come up with an action plan and let's start this fight today.*

As Cathy was going through her consultation notes, Joe was examining the pathology report to try to get an understanding of the test results. It was during this time of the report examination that he learned that the situation was worse than he had initially thought. The test of Cathy's blood cells showed that of the 2,000 blood cells that were tested, over 94.3 percent of the cells were cancer cells (X), so basically 94 percent of her blood was cancer. This information was going to remain his personal secret for at least the next eight months. However, it was no secret that Cathy was in for the battle of her life, and he needed to find a way to make sure this was one fight she was going to win. He had no clue what he was going to do, but it was apparent that he needed to develop an action plan immediately. The one thing he was confident of was that he was not going to sit around and wait to see what the outcome was going to be.

The next morning started bright and early, with tests being done and scheduled surgery to insert a port in her chest that would serve as a delivery port for the chemo to be inserted into her body for the next eight months.

After a refresher consultation, the order for the first batch of chemo was sent down to the lab to be created. Since there are many types and variations of chemo to treat the types of cancers, each batch of chemo had to be designed exclusively for the individual to be treated. The wait allowed Cathy to once again think about what was about to happen, and the fear and anxiety returned at a heightened level that she had never experienced before.

As she sat with Joe, they both shared her fears and tears. However, her husband knew that this was the time and opportunity to launch the first phase of his plan of action. He stood and looked into his wife's eyes and told her that he was scared as well and very sorry for what was happening to her. Joe said to her that if he could, he would change places with her in a heartbeat, but he was out of the magic dust that would let that type of thing happen. He told her that it was time for her to get mad and launch that stubborn German temper that she had. The same stubbornness that she had used on him for the past forty years.

He told her that she was in for the fight of her life, and he was going to be at her side the whole way, coaching, comforting, and soothing her fears every step of the way. It was a fight that they were going to win together, but he could not do it alone. He needed her to fight like a girl, and their chances of winning this fight would be in their favor. He stated that from this day forward, there would be no talk of dying or losing this battle. The only thing that they would do was talk about living and what they were going to do when she was better.

Joe sat down next to Cathy and said, "Let us take a minute and look back on how much we have accomplished in life together." He reminded her that they were merely teenagers when they were married, and no one believed that their marriage would last. In spite of the continuous interference and criticism from both family members and outsiders, they had accomplished more than anyone ever gave them credit for. They had not only had forty years of a great life together, but they had also raised three sons that have made them very proud.

Joe looked in Cathy's eyes and said, "Together we have overcome every challenge we faced in life, and this new challenge will be no different. It may take every ounce of energy we have, but we will win." Joe told Cathy, not only how much he loved her, but how much her three sons loved her. He then threw in his secret weapon, and he told her how much her grandchildren loved her and how her granddaughter was waiting for her to teach her to be a top-notch cheerleader, have sleepovers together, and watch her walk down the aisle someday. Losing was no longer an option in this fight; the only option was to win. He also told her that they were going to have a slogan for this fight, and it was going to be "No One Fights Alone," and all of her friends, family, and coworkers were in this fight with her and would be until victory was hers.

Cathy wiped her tears away from her cheeks. She knew that her partner was right and that she had no doubt that he would be at her side for however long it took to win this fight facing them. They spent the remaining time in each other's arms, and each one secretly thought about how they were going to pull this off.

As Joe was driving home that evening, he realized that it was time for him to come up with the next step of whatever he was going to do in his new, unexpected role of being the caregiver of his wife during her upcoming fight. It was at this time of deep thought he realized that he would not be able to do this alone; he needed to create a support team that was like no other support team. His support and coaching of Cathy would eventually grow old and redundant over the next eight months or so. How many times does a person want to hear the same person telling them to fight, be strong, stay positive, don't give up, and never stop believing? He realized that he needed to bring to fruition the theme "No One Fights Alone" and involve all of their friends and family as the devoted support team that would be a crucial part in allowing Cathy to feel the love and support that will get her through those tough moments or low points that were sure to be a significant challenge during this long and tiring fight that she was going to face.

When Joe arrived home, he phoned his sons and brought them up to speed on everything that happened and was going to happen. He had told them there would be daily updates on Cathy's condition and treatment. He then called his next-door neighbor, for she was a very dear friend to both him and Cathy. As luck would have it, she was home, and he told her about Cathy's illness. A few minutes after they ended their call, the neighbor's husband came over to the house. He informed

Joe that they would be there for him and Cathy, and the neighbors would band together and do all of the landscaping chores, and anything else that would need to be done, for Joe's job was to take care of Cathy. So, for the next three months, the neighbors took shifts on cutting the lawn, trimming the hedges/bushes, and the neighbor three doors down planted flowers in the backyard.

There was still one phone call that needed to be made. Cathy and her sister in Virginia shared the responsibility of caring for her ninety-eight-year-old mother. Her mother had recently left Florida to spend the next six months in Virginia. After a brief discussion with Joe, Cathy agreed that she would call her mother and break the news of her new challenge. After a lengthy conversation with her mother, Cathy was able to convince her that getting on a plane and flying back to Florida would not be in the best interest of Cathy, Joe, and the medical team. When Cathy hung up from her mother, her heart was sad and heavy. Having sons of her own, she understood the love of a mother and her child, and how important it was for a mother to be with her child during a time of sickness and hardship. It broke Cathy's heart to take the tough love approach but was best for everyone.

3.

Cathy's husband realized that the time had come to bring everyone up to date on the current diagnosis of Cathy's illness. He knew that there were coworkers, family members, family friends, and neighbors who needed to be updated, and he needed to figure out a way to get the message out in a timely fashion.

After considering his options, he decided that he would create an email publication titled "Cathy's Corner." On July 8, the first publication of "Cathy's Corner No One Fights Alone" went out to eighteen people to notify them of Cathy's illness and the schedule of treatments. Cathy had heard later that when the H.R. person at her workplace forwarded it out to all of the employees, "you could hear a pin drop" as all activities ceased immediately. Everyone stopped to read "Cathy's Corner." Many of her coworkers had tear-filled eyes, shortly after the tears subsided, Cathy's support team started to materialize. Her husband purchased orange, the designated color for leukemia, wristbands that read "No One Fights Alone," along with orange fabric apparel ribbons that had an adhesive on the back so anyone could place it on just about anything they would like, including their clothes. For the next two years, Cathy's support team wore their wristbands and apparel ribbons proudly as they prayed for her to win her fight against this horrible monster.

After experiencing the overwhelming love and support that was coming Cathy's way from her friends and family, Joe knew that Cathy's Corner was going to be a significant part of Cathy's motivation and inspiration to come out a winner in her fight. He also realized that it would be extremely beneficial for Cathy if she were the one writing *Cathy's Corner*. However, with all that she had going on with her chemo treatment and possible side effects, it was apparent she would not be up to the task of writing *Cathy's Corner*. Therefore, her husband decided that he would become the ghostwriter for *Cathy's Corner*, writing every publication in the first person and having Cathy edit and proofread the final copy before he emailed it out to her support team.

It did not take long for Joe to realize that he had a significant challenge before him. He not only had to find a way to help beat a vicious monster called **CANCER**, but he now had to learn quickly how to think like a *WOMAN* so he could write *Cathy's Corner* effectively.

After being married for forty years, he quickly realized that he knew his wife as well as she knew herself, so the writing of *Cathy's Corner* became an enjoyable activity that he looked forward to creating twice a month. As word about Cathy's challenge spread, the list of people that wanted to be included on the mailing list of *Cathy's Corner* grew to an astonishing 100+ people, and that does not include the number of people each email was forwarded to from the original recipients. *Cathy's Corner* reached people all over the country—Salt Lake City, Los Angeles, Chicago, Troy, MI, and Connecticut.

The first being the week she went into the hospital to start her two-week chemo treatment. The second was written when she checked out of the hospital and went home to regain her strength so she could return to the hospital for another two weeks of chemo. Each publication of *Cathy's*

Corner started with a recap of her treatment, the hardships and side effects, Cathy's thoughts and comments.

The next section was usually photos of Cathy, her friends, and her family. Some were of her three sons when they were little boys, and there were photos of her sons as young adults. Then the grandkids' photos started showing up. When September came (which is the National Month for Leukemia Awareness), people would send emails of themselves wearing orange shirts or other apparel in support of her fight. There was a photo of four of Cathy's coworkers wearing orange T-shirts, and when they stood together, their shirts spelled out, "NO ONE FIGHTS ALONE," there were photos of Cathy's supporters' children wearing orange apparel to school in her honor. One of her coworkers sewed together a large quilt titled "No One Fights Alone," and every employee signed their name in one of the squares of the quilt. Before they sent the quilt to Cathy, they all went outside of the building and hung the quilt from the second-floor balcony, then went down to the first floor and had a group photo taken under the quilt.

Of course, the photo was in a future publication of *Cathy's Corner*. In the next section of *Cathy's Corner*, two motivational quotes covered various topics about life, fighting cancer, and friends and family, followed by three song selections that tied into the theme of the current publication. Songs such as "I am Woman" by Helen Reddy, "Believe" by Cher, "Strong Enough" by Cher, songs by REO Speedwagon, Lynyrd Skynyrd, Alabama, Molly Hatchet, Motley Crew, Grand Funk Railroad, Doobie Brothers, and Carrie Underwood to name a few. There were times supporters would email songs they thought could be featured in a future *Cathy's Corner*.

Each publication would end:
Love and Prayers
Ms. Cathy
Keeping the Prayers on High Beam

CATHY'S CORNER

Cathy's Corner "No One Fights Alone"- 7-11-2013
A small victory... a day to celebrate

Well... day three is going well. I have had four types of chemo treatments so far and have two left to go for phase one of our plan of attack. Also, part of the treatment process is to remove fluid from your spine and analyze for cancer cells. Well... the results are back, and there is no sign of cancer cells in my spinal fluid. **HOORAY!!!!!!!!** It appears that we caught this monster early enough.

The other good news is my swollen salivary glands and blood pressure have returned to normal. I am having a good day.

Once again, I thank everyone for the continuous prayers and support. You make every day extraordinary for me.

Q&A

Q. *Can we send flowers?*

A. As you know, I love flowers and the beauty they bring. However, I have learned that, as of today, I am not allowed to have flowers or plants in my room. My white blood cells are getting low and will get lower before they build me back up.

Therefore, my immune system is deficient, and I am very vulnerable. Just your love and prayers are enough for now.

Cathy's Daily Message:
Listen to the birds sing and try to whistle back.

Today's Song:

"Celebration"...Kool and the gang.

"Devil Went Down to Georgia"...Jamison Celtic Rock

Cathy's Corner "No One Fights Alone" 7-18-2013
TGIF #2...the end of my second week.

As the second week comes to an end, I very happy to say that it has been a good week. The best news is that I had my last chemo treatment on Thursday evening. The next step is for my nursing team to start the build-up process with the platelets and white blood cells. Once we get both of those in the order, I can get to go home. Not quite sure how long I will be able to stay home before I come back to start phase two of the treatment program.

I am soooooooooooooooooo looking forward to going home, sleeping in my bed and walking through my house and not eating dinner @ 4:30 every day.

I know that I am repeating myself, but I want everyone to know how much I appreciate your love, prayers, and, most importantly, your friendship. I cannot say enough about the heartwarming feeling I get with all of your love and support. We are going to win this battle together.

I wish everyone to have a great weekend, and hopefully, you will get to spend time with family and loved ones. My youngest son Jaison from Atlanta is in town with his family, so I know that I will be having a great weekend.

Cathy's Daily Suggestion:
Try to find time this weekend to enjoy a Sunrise and/or Sunset. Hopefully, with a particular person in your life.

Today's Song:
"The South is Going to Do it Again"...Charlie Daniels Band

"Battleship Chains"...Georgia Satellites

Today's photo is a photo of Joe and me at our favorite hiking spot.

The photo was taken at Rim Rock overlook in the Allegheny National Forest in northwestern Pennsylvania.

Cathy's Corner "No One Fights Alone" July 21, 2013
Week #3...As we continue to meet the challenge.
I hope everyone had a great weekend. I enjoyed my time with my son Jaison and his wife. Due to the state of my white blood cells, I was unable to see the grandchildren in person. But I did Skype numerous times over the weekend. So, I was able to spend a reasonable amount of time with them. They are getting more beautiful every day.

Update—very little has changed since my last *Cathy's Corner*. The chemo treatment for this phase is over (and I only have five more to go... UUUGH), and my team of nurses are working on building me back up. I did have a small bump in the road with mouth sores from the chemo, and it appears I have turned the Corner and feeling better. So... now to get to the point—I can go home for a short stay before we begin the phase two treatment.

I have received many get well cards and text messages; please know that I appreciate everyone taking time out of their day to think of me. You are all special to me.

I want to say a special **Thank You** to my friends and family at work. I understand that you have a blood drive scheduled on my behalf for August 1. Words cannot express my appreciation and gratitude for your loving care.

There would be nothing better than getting blood from my family and friends.

Jaison's Surprise!!!!!! As you know, I am not allowed to have flowers or plants at this stage of my treatment. So, my son Jaison made me fifty-six paper flowers (one for each year of my life) with pictures in the center of the flowers covering from the time all three boys were babies to today's grandchildren. Fifty-six years of great times and memories of raising three boys. Now, the real kicker is that forty-four buds have yet to bloom. Therefore as we move forward in life, we will add a picture a year. After a lengthy discussion on the sum of 56 + 44, we decided that we will open two buds each year for a while.

Cathy's Message of the Day:
Share a smile with five different people

Song of the Day:

"The House is a Rocking"...Stevie Ray Vaughn

"Let It Rock"...Georgia Satellites

Today's Special Hello goes to my granddaughter, our little Georgia Peach... she is now one month old.

Cathy's Corner "No One Fights Alone" 07-26-2013
TGIF...X 2

Well, it is another Friday, and I hope everyone is planning to do something fun this weekend. You are probably wondering why I did an X2 on my heading, well... the x 2 means that it is a TGIF for you and me. **I GOT TO GO HOME LAST NIGHT (Thursday) FROM THE HOSPITAL.** The doctor came in yesterday and said that my white blood cell count has jumped up tremendously; it was like I was superwoman (hmm, so does that mean that Kryptonite affects my leukemia?) So today is my first Friday at home since July 3. Boy, does it feel sooo good to sleep in my bed. I have to see the doctor on Monday for a checkup. I hope that she will be able to tell me then what my schedule will be for phase two of treatment. I think that I will be home for about a week then back to the hospital for phase two, which should last two weeks.

It is a good thing that Joe likes to cook because I am still getting the Royal Treatment in the nutrition area. His cooking is much better than hospitals.

I am still feeling tired, but I have learned to pace myself, and I am getting proper rest. (on *my* couch and in *my* bed.)

I will keep everyone updated on my schedule and timing of events as I learn them.

Again thank you for all of your prayers and get-well wishes, I re-read the cards and written messages over and over.

Cathy's Suggestion of the day:
Smile and say hello to five unknown people you meet/see in your travels this weekend. You will be surprised at how good you will feel at the end of the day.

Today's Song:
"Pride & Joy"...Stevie Ray Vaughan

"Dixieland Delight"...Alabama

Today's photo (from Joe) is a picture of Cathy with her trademark smile. The photo was taken last Christmas (2012), and the older lady on the right side of the photo is her mother, who turned ninety-seven this past May.

4.

On the second day of phase one, chemo treatment was about to begin as Joe arrived to be at her side. As he entered the hospital room, he was taken by surprise at the sight of his wife. While he was away, she had gone down to the hospital salon and had them shave off her shoulder-length hair, and now she was down to a head of hair that resembled a man's three-day beard. As he was staring at her, she smiled and said that "there was no way I was going to sit here and watch my hair fall out in clumps over the next three weeks. It is bad enough I am going to lose every hair on my body, including my eyelashes and eyebrows but, watching the hair on my head fall out in clumps would only depress me to a level that I don't want to go to." Her husband just smiled and said, "I think you look great and remember true beauty is your heart, not your body." They kissed each other hello and discussed the schedule and happenings of the day.

Much to their surprise, Cathy's petite 5 body was handling the chemo treatment better than the medical team had expected. There were side effects like continuously being tired, but everything was manageable. Her biggest struggle came when she went to the surgical room for the spinal tap. This was where they would stick a six-inch needle into the base of her back and into the spine to extract spinal fluid. She could feel that needle enter her back, and feel it as it entered her spine. One time they hit a nerve, and she thought that she was going to jump off the table and end up on the ceiling. The thought that they were going to do this procedure for at least six times did not make her a happy camper. She talked with her oncologist about her fear, and they concluded that they would sedate her every time so she would be more relaxed and handle the procedure better. Not doing the procedure was not an option since it was needed to make sure that cancer had not spread to the spine, for if it did, that meant that it would eventually go to her brain.

The chemo treatment continued as scheduled for the next ten days as Cathy and her husband passed the time playing cards, a new board game named Sequence, and watching Amazon Prime and Netflix shows on Cathy's laptop, such as *Justified*, *Greys Anatomy* and *24*, Then on day seventeen, the medical team announced this round of treatment had concluded, and it was time to get her prepared to go home and build back up so she can return in two weeks to begin the process all over again.

The medical team explained to Cathy that the next step was to inject her with Neupogen, which is a Filgrastim injection that is used to treat neutropenia (low white blood cells) that is caused by cancer treatments. It is a synthetic form of a substance known as colony stimulating factor, which the body naturally produces. Filgrastim helps the bone marrow to make new white blood cells. Common side effects of Neupogen include aching or pain in the bones and muscles, diarrhea, constipation, hair loss, headache, tired feeling, skin rash, nosebleeds, or injection site reactions (redness, swelling, itching, lumps, or bruising).

Being that the chemo had killed all of the white blood cells in her body and she did not have an immune system, and it was important that before she left the hospital that her white blood count needed to be a minimum of 5.0. If, for some reason, she would get a virus or infection, she would not be able to fight it, which meant she would not be around to see her grandchildren.

When Cathy was cleared to go home and recuperate from round one of treatment and get her body ready for round two, which was scheduled in about two weeks, she had quite a list of chores and tasks that were needed to be completed before her return to the hospital. Cathy was determined to cross everything off her list before she returned to the hospital.

The first item on her list was to thoroughly sanitize her home from top to bottom, leaving no carpet, rug, wall, shelf, counter, or bathroom untouched. There were a few situations where some locations were cleaned more than once, and the phrase "Kills 99.8% germs" was on every cleaning product that was used. The other items on her list included meeting with an attorney to complete her last will and testament; she knew that 98% of everything would go to her husband. Still, she wanted to cover all the bases legally as well as creating a list that would show a detailed disbursement of her personal property and who the recipients would be, such as her three sons, daughters-in-law, and most importantly her grandchildren.

Those hours she spent performing the task, as mentioned above, was the most challenging and heartbreaking task that she would ever do in her life. But somehow, Cathy found the courage and tenacity to complete the task as she prayed long and hard that it would be a repeating task that, in the end, would prove to be unnecessary. Working through her list with her husband by her side, together, they chipped away at everything that needed to be completed before she returned to the hospital. As the list was nearing completion, they stopped and reflected on all of the things that they had done together in the past weeks to accomplish the tasks at hand. They talked about how they were going to win this fight and, life was going to be as good in the future as it was before she got sick.

Little did they know that this time next week, they would be faced with an unexpected setback that could evaporate their dreams of victory in a blink of the eye.

Perhaps, if there indeed was a silver lining to what was happening in Cathy's life was that her husband would be there for her for as long as it took to beat this vicious monster called cancer. At the time of her sickness, Joe was an independent manufacturer's representative. He represented consumer products for three different manufacturers calling on the headquarters of the major retailers in the US. Being self-employed meant that he worked from an office at his residence with the ability to create his schedule to cover the needs of each manufacturer and retailer. With Cathy's situation, he notified his clients and was extremely pleased when they said that they would be there for him and support him as long as it took to get his wife healthy again, in fact, all three clients became an ongoing recipient of *Cathy's Corner*.

With the support from his clients, He was able to limit his out of town travel as well as starting his days very early in the morning and ending them in the early afternoon, for this would enable him to be with Cathy each evening. On weekdays he would be at the hospital from around 4:00 p.m. until 9:30, and on the weekends, he would be there from around 1:30 p.m. until 9:30 p.m. But one thing was certain, except for the few times he was out of town for work-related trips, Cathy never ate dinner alone. Her husband would always bring dinner with him, and they would sit together and have dinner and discuss the happenings of the day. Sometimes on the weekends, he would make dinner for both of them (this would allow Cathy a break from the hospital food). The hospital staff would always stop by Cathy's room to enjoy the aroma of Joe's home-cooked meal and see what was on the menu that day.

On Saturday afternoons, Cathy and Joe watched college football together, and sometimes nurse Dan would come in and sit with them to catch up on the scores. The only problem was that nurse Dan was a fan of Ohio State, but they did not hold that against him and prayed that someday he would see the light and join them as they cheered for Penn State. During the week, they played card games, board games, watched movies, and TV series like *Justified* and *24* on Cathy's laptop, and there were the evenings they would sit and write *Cathy's Corner* together. Somehow, Joe always had a way of saying what Cathy felt in her heart or wanted to say that touched the readers just the way Cathy wanted it.

They also kept their promise to each other, and they never once talked about Cathy losing her fight. They always talked about what they were going to do when she was better and the fun things they were going to with the grandkids as they are growing up. Every day started with a smile and ended with a kiss.

The time had come for them to return to the hospital to begin treatment number two of eight. Cathy and her husband were anxious to get Cathy admitted into the hospital and to get the next round of chemo started so that they can go back home as quickly as possible. However, little did they know that going home was not going to happen as they had planned.

The nurses and doctors greeted Cathy with bright smiles and friendly hellos. The hospital staff knew that it was never a pleasant experience for a person to be returning to the oncology unit and they made every effort to make their patients feel comfortable and help them obtain the peace of mind that would allow them to experience as pleasant a time with the medical team as possible.

The nurses wasted no time preparing Cathy for her next chemo treatment. As they were trying to insert the needle into the port that was located under her skin at the right side of her chest, they were having difficulty finding the correct location of the port that would allow the needle to be inserted without harm to the patient. After numerous attempts from three different nurses, they concluded that there was a problem, and they needed to call up a specialist that was more familiar with the ports used for chemo patients. After a thorough examination of Cathy's situation, they discovered that there were two problems.

The first was that the port had somehow turned or shifted and was not in the correct position, and the second problem was that there appeared to be some type of infection that was present around the scar where they had surgically inserted the port. So now they had two problems at hand, and both needed to be resolved before chemo treatment could begin. The infection was the priority due to the fact that Cathy's immune system was at an extremely low level, and an infection could race through her body like a wildfire, which in turn would result in an unexpected ending to her fight of beating her monster and extending her stay on this earth.

The infectious disease team told Cathy that there was no way to tell how her port became infected. Perhaps it could have been as simple as bacteria from a showerhead, as was common in central Florida homes. The infectious disease team quickly reacted and started administering an aggressive antibiotic that would hopefully attack the infection quickly and effectively. After the medicines started flowing into Cathy's body, the medical team moved their thoughts to the problem relating to the misaligned port in her chest. As they began to discuss the possible courses of action that were before them, the one thing they did agree on was the current port needed to be replaced, but where to surgically insert its replacement? There was the talk of putting the replacement port on the left side of her chest, but there was a serious concern that the chemo being injected in her body would be too close to the heart.

Unfortunately, one of the side effects of chemotherapy is that it not only destroys your cells but can be destroying your organs as well. Chemo treatments that end a life because of the side effects of a person's organs failing were not uncommon. Cathy's oncologist came into the meeting of the minds and stated that the port on the left side of the chest was not an option that she would approve and advised them that they needed to come up with a better solution, and please come up with it quickly. After further discussion, the medical team came up with the solution that Dr. Lukeman found acceptable. They would remove the existing port and reinsert the new one about 4 – 6 inches higher on the right side of the chest. The surgical team waited for three days to allow the antibiotics to perform their job effectively. Then they completed the task of removing the old port and inserting a replacement. Cathy then had to wait another three days to make sure that there were no complications, and the infection was completely gone. After the extended wait, the nurses were given the green light to resume Cathy's second month of treatment.

The rest of the treatment process went uneventfully, and after spending a few days building her white blood cell count up to 5.0, she was released to go home and build herself back up so she could return to start the process all over again.

Cathy's Corner "No One Fights Alone" 8-5-2013
Happy Monday..............The adventure continues.
Treatment # 2

I hope everyone had a great weekend. Mine was fantastic, My son Bob and his wife Megan came in from Pittsburgh to visit for four days, and we had a great time. Joe Jr. and his wife came over, which made the weekend very special. Bob used some of his new recipes to make dinners for the weekend, and they were delicious. It was a weekend filled with smiles, laughs, and excitement. Unfortunately, it went too fast and was over in a blink of an eye.

I checked back into the hospital Sunday afternoon to start preparing for the next phase of chemo treatment (Phase B). I learned that there are two phases of chemo treatment for my leukemia. Each phase has a different recipe for chemo. Phase A will be done on chemo treatment 1,3,5,7, and Phase B will be done on chemo treatment 2,4,6,8. If everything works according to plan, and the results are positive, the procedures may end after treatment # 6. It is a wait-and-see process.

The plan of attack appears that I should be in the hospital for the first two weeks of each month and then sent home to recover the last two weeks of each month. So needless to say, this phase that I am having now will be a new type of chemo for me. I am keeping my fingers crossed that I do as well with this one as I did with the first one.

I want to thank everyone for the cards, emails, and text messages. You are the best friends a person can hope for. I was looking on a leukemia website (Choose Hope) and learned that the color ribbon for leukemia is orange. I also discovered two sayings that I liked, the first was "Fight like a girl" (which is easy for me), and the second was "No One Fights Alone." The second hit home due to the fact that from the time of my diagnosis, I have never felt that I was fighting this battle alone. Everyone has been fighting alongside me the entire time. You have no idea how it feels to be cared for by so many people. I greatly appreciate your support and commitment to my battle. I know many people with cancer have a support team, but somehow I feel that I have a support team that is second to none. You are all loved dearly.

Well... this concludes my *Cathy's Corner* update and I will probably do an update Friday to wish everyone a good weekend. Let's pray for a good week of treatment.

Cathy's suggestion of the day:
Wear something orange this week.

Today's Song :

(I am in somewhat of a nostalgic mood, so we are going back to Motown. Those of you that are my age will remember growing up some of these songs and those of you that are younger might remember your parents singing to these tunes. Anyways, I hope they bring back good memories.)

"You are My Everything"... The Temptations

"Get Ready"... The Temptations

Photo of the day (from Joe) (since we are being nostalgic, today's photo is of Cathy and her youngest son Jaison at six years old, when she lived in Utah. The second photo was Cathy and Jaison when he received his master's degree from Auburn University in 2010.

Cathy and Jaison

Cathy's Corner "No one Fights Alone" 8-9-2013
TGIF...A week with a bump in the road.

Well, what can I say, some of the best-laid plans seem to not go according to a person's intentions and wishes? I checked into the hospital Sunday afternoon with a positive attitude to begin my next phase of chemo treatment. Then the plan of attack changed before I knew what was going on. I developed a fever during the night on Sunday, which constituted the doctors to do a blood analysis to see what caused the fever. Wouldn't you know it, my port developed an infection, and all chemo treatment was put on hold until we can get the virus out of my system.

They ended up removing the port that they had inserted in my chest, and I have been treated with antibiotics all week. It appears that the infection is finally leaving, and I will be on antibiotics over the weekend to make sure there are no lingering germs. So needless to say, I have lost a whole week of chemo treatment. Hopefully, we can get back on track Monday of next week. It was nothing real severe but serious enough that we had to take aggressive measures to get back on track. The good news was that they did a CAT scan, and the results showed that my lymph nodes are shrinking, which means that the chemo is working so far.

Oh well, a little bump in the road, and now we are heading down the right parkway.

So that you know, your prayers from last week were not wasted... they just went to another cause.

I received a lovely gift basket from my family this week that was themed to leukemia and the color orange. The gift basket contained a baseball cap with the orange ribbon, coffee mug, orange wristband that said, "No One Fights Alone," a key chain, a bookmarker, an orange water bottle, an enamel pin, and a few other goodies. The one item that hit home was the bookmarker that listed ten things that cancer cannot do. I want to share these with you starting today and in the upcoming Cathy's Corner.

Well, that is my update for this week. I hope that I have positive news next week relating to my chemo treatment. Now that I am 98% bald, I am ready to get this thing moving along and behind me as soon as possible.

I received some text messages and photos of people wearing orange this week. Thank you! I appreciate it.

Cathy's comment:
What Cancer Cannot Do—**Cancer is so limited. It Cannot Cripple Hope**

Today's song is a TGIF special:
"Dancing in the Streets"...Martha Reeves and the Vandellas

"Heat Wave"...Martha Reeves and the Vandellas

Today's Special "You are the Best" goes to:
My friends/coworkers from our Lakeland Florida office holding four poster boards spelling out "NO ONE FIGHTS ALONE" in orange print, sharing their support for me.

Thanks, you made my day.

Until the next Cathy's Corner
Love & Prayers
Ms. Cathy

Cathy's Corner "No One Fights alone" 8-13-2013
Happy Tuesday... Back on the right track!!!!!!!

I hope everyone had a lovely weekend. I understand that it has been scorching, and the rains are slow coming. Oh well, welcome to the dog days of summer.

I had a good weekend, the antibiotics did their job, and the infection has been eliminated. Now back to our task at hand... Killing Mr. Leukemia.

Looking back, it appears that the infection was a blessing in disguise. The extra time that was required to fight the infection gave my body a chance to get stronger. Dr. Lukeman was very excited to learn that my platelets are up to 135 (normal is 140-150). You have to remember that when I was diagnosed with leukemia, my platelets were 14, and I had to have platelets added to my blood three different times to get up to an acceptable level (my highest number was 90).

My blood count is normal, and my white blood cells are healthy. I am at my strongest point in three months as I take on this next phase of chemo treatment. Dr. Lukeman has decided that she wants to do another port instead of the PICC. I had the port inserted this morning, and chemo will begin this afternoon. All of those good numbers are going to go away, but that is the way chemo works.

WE ARE BACK ON TRACK

I have received some emails with photos showing your support, and I **LOVE** them. I will include all of the images in Cathy's Corner so everyone can see how great you people are. You know, Cathy's Corner has nationwide coverage. I have people in the east to Fairfield, CT., and Auburn, NY. North to Chicago, IL, and Michigan, west to Salt Lake City, UT, and Orange County, CA. I am truly blessed with some of the best friends a person could hope to have.

Well, that wraps it up for my latest update. I will post again on Friday or Saturday morning.

Cathy's Comment of the day:
What Cancer Cannot Do—**Cancer is so limited... IT CANNOT SHATTER HOPE**

Today's Song:

Dedicated to Mr. Leukemia—"No where to Run"... Martha Reeves and the Vandellas

A bluegrass favorite—"Oh, What a Love"...Nitty Gritty Dirt Band

Love & Prayers
Ms. Cathy

Cathy's Corner "No One Fights Alone" 8-19-2013
TGIF… The end of a productive week

As I stated in my last email, the infection finally left, the new port was surgically implanted in my chest, and phase two of the chemo program was started on Tuesday and completed by early next week. Then I start the rebuild process so I can home and rest. Then in about two weeks, we start the next round of chemo. So far, the side effects have been minimal, and I am praying that it stays that way. Dr. Lukeman is thrilled with the way everything is progressing. The only problem is that the infection set me back a week in my timetable for treatment. I will now be in the hospital for the second and third week of each month. Instead of the first and second week. The scheduling is still in my favor for being home for Thanksgiving and Christmas. I hope and pray that there are no more setbacks.

I know that I have an excellent doctor and hospital staff, but I contribute my progress to P.O.P. (POWER OF PRAYS). I thank everyone every day in my prayers for their never-ending support and prayers. We have eight mountains to climb and are starting our descent on mountain two, where we will rest at the bottom and then begin our climb up mountain three etc. Etc.

Q&A

Q. if everything progresses at the same rate as the first two treatments is there a chance that you will not have all 6-8 treatments?

A. Unfortunately, NO. There are no shortcuts or time off early for good behavior. The real problem is that the cancer cells are produced in the bone marrow. Even though it appears the bone marrow may not be producing cancer cells, you cannot stop treatment until you do at least six months of chemo to make sure that cancer in the bone marrow is nonexistent. There needs to be undeniable proof that the bone marrow is not creating cancer cells and sending them to your blood. After six months of chemo, they will do another bone marrow specimen to make sure that there is no sign of cancer cells. If there is any doubt, then we will go for another two months and then do another bone marrow to confirm the status. I am very confident that we will beat this monster in the first six months. Then my hair will grow back, I will go to Atlanta to see my grandkids and return to my family at The Mortgage Firm. **LIFE WILL BE GOOD AGAIN....**

I had a few coworkers come and see me this week, and I enjoyed their company. It is so lovely to spend time with friends and family. I had the chance to test a few of my scarves and hats this week to cover up my cold head. I am enjoying trying out my selection of scarves.

Cathy's Comment of the day:
What Cancer Cannot Do—**Cancer is so limited... it cannot destroy faith**

Today's song:
We are going to put an upbeat step in our weekend and shake a little booty with:

"Footstompimg Music"...Grand Funk Railroad

"Whole Lotts Shakin'"...Georgia Satellites

Since everyone enjoyed my nostalgia with Jaison when he was a little boy, we are going back to Utah when our three boys were playing hockey, and we were one big hockey family. We were at ice rinks more than we were home.

Cathy's Corner "No One Fights Alone" 8-23-2013
TGIF (depending on when you are reading this)...
Homeward Bound

Everything is moving along nicely. My white cells are back up to 4.0 (which is normal), and I am continuing my Neupogen shots to keep the production of white blood cells going strong. The doctor is making sure I am progressing in the right direction, and there is no chance of crashing. If everything looks good Friday morning, it seems like I will get to go home Friday afternoon. YEA!! YEA!! YEA!! So let us all keep our fingers crossed and pray for a Good Friday.

I have a few **COOL** happenings to share with you that happened this week.

COOL HAPPENING # 1—Due to the chemo treatment, my blood level started dropping, so I had to be given blood, and guess what? I was looking at the label on the bag of blood, and I noticed I was getting blood that was donated in my name, and it happened to be from my youngest son, Jaison. **HOW COOL IS THAT???** It made me happy and proud to be getting blood from my son. Then to make it a double **COOL HAPPENING,** I was given a second bag of blood that same night, and when I looked at the label, I saw that the blood was donated in my name from Denise Van Pelt a friend and coworker of mine. So between Jaison and Denise, my blood is looking great.

COOL HAPPENING # 2—My employer bought some bracelets that were leukemia orange and had the sayings: **WE'RE IN THIS TOGETHER** and **HOPE, FAITH, LOVE.** They had some leftover and gave them to Joe so we could share with our friends and family. They also included a unique bracelet, especially for me, that is shaped like a cross with clear crystals and orange beads. It is beautiful and an extraordinary bracelet. **NOW, HOW COOL IS THAT?**

COOL HAPPENING # 3—One of our neighbors

went into our backyard and planted new flowers in our four flower pots that border our pool. Guess what kind of flowers they planted? **ORANGE MARIGOLDS... NOW, HOW COOL IS THAT?** Our neighbors have been a big part of my support team, and I appreciate everything they do for Joe and me.

Cathy's comment of the day:
What Cancer Cannot Do—**Cancer is so limited. It cannot eat away peace.**

Today's song. Since we will be taking a break from Cathy's Corner until our next hospital visit, we are going to feature three songs.

The first is to put a boogey in your step— "Jump, Shout Boogie"...Barry Manilow

The second is for my trip home— "Home Sweet Home"...Motley Crue

The third is for our Labor Day Friends— "All My Rowdy Friends are Coming Over Tonight"...Hank Williams, Jr.

Today's Photo is an exceptional photo featuring Cathy's mother, Maggie. Mom turned 98 on May 1st of this year, and she is still kicking butt. You will see that she is dressed in (leukemia) orange and is wearing her "No One Fights Alone" button, has her orange wristband on, and her appliques are on her walker. She is our oldest member of Cathy's Corner.

LOVE YOU, MOM. !!!!!!!!!!!!!!!!!!!!!

"NO ONE FIGHTS ALONE"
Love & Prayers
Ms. Cathy

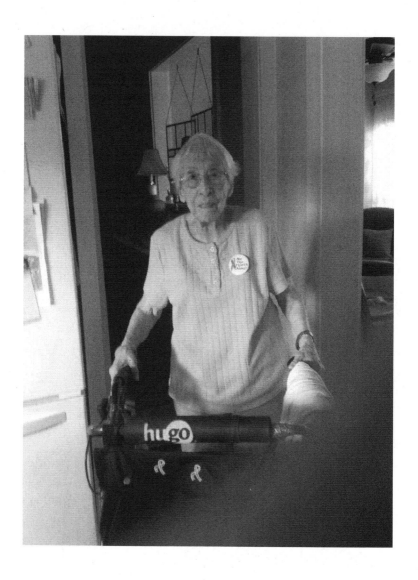

Cathy's Corner "No One Fights Alone" 9-12-2013
Happy Tuesday... I AM BACK AND READY TO CLIMB THE NEXT MOUNTAIN

I know many of you have been looking for the next Cathy's Corner, and I meant to have it out yesterday, but it took forever to get admitted into the hospital due to a lack of rooms. I was supposed to be admitted on Monday afternoon, but beds were scarce, and I did not get into a room until 9:30 p.m. Monday. By the time Joe and I got everything set up, we decided to call it a night and write the update today. I was hoping to get in my hospital room Sunday, but you have to start chemo precisely thirty days from the start of your last chemo treatment, which delayed everything a day. Well, it worked out because Joe and I went out and had a nice dinner and walked the mall by the hospital, and waited for the hospital to call.

So far, no infections or problems with chest port, so I am ready to go. Chemo started today; we are back to the Phase A treatment cycle (1,3,5), which is the more aggressive treatment cycle, which I have the most side effects to date. It appears that I am going to get three days of chemo to take a two-day break and then have two more days of chemo that includes two intrathecal procedures. (Chemo applied to the spine to prevent cancer cells from going to the brain) Since I went through this before, I am both mentally and physically ready to take this monster head-on. We will keep the prayers on high beam and tackle this as a team.

It was so great to be home as I was building myself back up to get ready for the next round of treatment. Joe and I spent some quality time together, and he made some delicious dinners. It was nice to eat some home cooking. We had some neighbors over for a little cookout on Labor Day, and it was so good to spend time with special friends. We spent a reasonable amount of time catching up on the past two months. What an enjoyable day.

Then to make it a double special week, I stopped at my place of employment after my doctor's appointment (which I passed with flying colors) and spent time with the best friends/coworkers a person could be blessed to have. I enjoyed my time with them and looked forward to seeing them again.

DO YOU KNOW WHAT SEPTEMBER IS??????? NO GUESS AGAIN.........OK, I WILL TELL YOU... **IT IS LEUKEMIA AWARENESS MONTH. It is an awareness month for 4-5 different types of cancers, but leukemia is the one closest to me.** I know there has been so much support for leukemia and me. I don't know what more we can do, but I am sure that some of you can put on your thinking caps and come up with some new unique ways to celebrate **LEUKEMIA AWARENESS MONTH. What I would be great would be to tell as many friends and family that September is LEUKEMIA AWARENESS Month and ask them to pick a particular time to wear something orange. (If you tell two people, and then they tell two people, and then they tell two people and before you know it, there would be thousands of new people aware of leukemia.)**

I have some more stories to share, but I will save them for the next Cathy's Corner.

Cathy's Comment of the day:
What Cancer Cannot Do—**Cancer is so limited. It cannot destroy confidence.**

Songs of the Day is a Triple Tuesday Special:
To Mr. Leukemia—"Strong Enough"...Cher

To the little road bumps—"ROLL WITH THE CHANGES"...REO SPEEDWAGON (Picked by my son Bob)

To My support team—"KEEP THE FIRE BURNIN'"...REO SPEEDWAGON

I am going to end with a heartwarming story. My friend and coworker's son was watching her get ready for work, and she was wearing orange as a day of support for me. He asks her why she was wearing orange, and she explained about leukemia and me and the color for leukemia being orange. After hearing the story, Tre' wanted to support my cause as well, and not only did he support my purpose, but he got a few of his friends to join him. They all wore orange shirts to school that day in my honor. THANK YOU!!!!

No One Fights Alone
Love and Prayers
Ms. Cathy

Cathy's Corner "No One Fights Alone" 9-15-2013
HAPPY MONDAY..................... TIME FOR A LITTLE BREAK.

Well... I have just completed four days of aggressive chemo (and I mean **AGGRESSIVE**). Even though you know what is coming at you, you still get knocked on your butt. I have never seen so many bags of chemo being administered; it was one bag after the other, nonstop for four days. I am holding up well, but still very tired and worn out. I swear, if this hospital had a blackout, no one would have a problem finding me; I would be the one glowing in the dark.

I now get a two-day break and try to get a little rest before we start one more day of chemo and one more intrathecal. Then, I will begin to work on building myself back up so I can home. The best thing is that after this treatment, we will be at the halfway mark. My support team has been in constant communication with me, and I am so thankful everyone is fighting this monster with me. I can never thank everyone enough for their love and prayers.

Before I left the hospital from my last treatment, my friend/coworker Rhonda Peek came to the hospital and presented me with a gift that she created especially for me. I was so surprised to see that she created a quilt with patchwork that said "Cathy's Comforter," and below that, it says "Get Well Soon," then there were individual messages and signatures from my friends from work. The gift was very heartwarming, and I had to hold back the tears of appreciation. The words were beautiful and inspiring. A Photo of the comforter is attached to this email so everyone can see it's beauty. Rhonda THANK YOU very much for taking the time to create a work of beauty. I will cherish it forever.

Leukemia Awareness Month Story: This story comes from our oldest son, Joe Jr. Joe is a manager at Chili's restaurant, and one night he had his server ask him about how the vegetables are cooked because there was a customer that could only have them a certain way. Joe Jr. went out to speak to the concerned customer and was quick to learn that she was a leukemia patient and needed to make sure that the vegetables are cooked all the way through. Joe explained that he understood and related his own experience with his mother and what she was going through. Joe also learned that the lady had completed her treatment and was now awaiting a bone marrow transplant. A few days later, the lady's daughter came and told Joe how good he made his mother feel and that she enjoyed his company. Now, how proud do you think I am??????

Cathy's Comment of the day:
What Cancer Cannot Do—**"Cancer is so limited....It Cannot Kill A Friendship"**

We are going to start the week with three fantastic songs for me. One about Angels and the other to get the blood flowing and foot tapping

Songs of the Day:
"ANGELS AMONG US"...ALABAMA

"IF YOU ARE GOING TO PLAY TEXAS (YOU GOT to HAVE A FIDDLE IN THE BAND)"... ALABAMA

"RAVE ON"...NITTY GRITTY DIRT BAND

In closing, I would like to give special hugs and kisses to my husband, Joe, who organizes and publishes Cathy's Corner for me when I am in treatment. He always helps me see the silver lining in the dark clouds.

The next edition of Cathy's Corner will be out Thursday/Friday

Love and Prayers...
Ms. Cathy

Cathy's Corner "No One Fights Alone" 9-25-2013
Home & Resting... Halfway to the Finish Line

My white blood cell count reached 7.1 (I needed to get to 4.0 to be able to come home), and the doctor released me to go home today. They gave me a bag of platelets and two bags of blood yesterday, which helped build me up along with the Neupogen shots. I am so glad to be home, out of pajamas, and I am looking forward to sleeping in my bed. I go to the oncologist on Friday the 27th to have my blood analyzed, which will enable them to see where all of my counts are. I am keeping my fingers crossed that everything stays on track. I will probably return to the hospital around October 8 or 9 to begin round 4 of 6 chemo treatment. I am still fatigued from the last treatment, but I should be getting a little stronger each day.

My birthday was adorable and unique even though I was in the hospital. Joe had a particular pull apart cake from Publix (made out of cupcakes, see attached photo) that I shared with all of the nurses on the day and night shift (about twenty people) and **BOY** were they happy campers. I received some great birthday cards from my family and friends. I was given a beautiful wooden angel from my friends Diane and Jamie, as well as a very fragrant candle from my friend Ivy. Joe brought dinner in, and we had a nice dinner and then watched a movie on the computer. It turned out to be a special day, and of course, I cried over all of the attention.

Thanks to everyone who played a part in making this day special.

Q&A Can you explain Neutropenia and Neupogen shots.

Neutropenia is when your white blood cells are so low you cease to have any immunity against bacteria or infection. This is one of the critical side effects of aggressive chemotherapy treatment. Once you become neutropenia, you must wear a mask and/or have everyone around you wear a mask.

Neupogen shots are administered to you (which are painful) to trick the body into aggressively producing white blood cells. The injection can take three days or longer, depending on the amount of chemo still in your bloodstream. The most significant risk throughout the whole process is infection. If you get any virus or infection, it could be life-threatening due to you have no white blood cells to fight for you.

My mother and sister sent me a cute little bear named Noah. He is wearing a T-shirt that says "Feel Better because when you feel better, I feel better."When you push on his hand, he begins to talk and tells you a short story about how special you are and how much he wants you to feel better. Needless to say, it gave me the Boo-hoo's when I first listened to it.

Cathy's Comment of the Day:
What Cancer Cannot Do—**"Cancer is so Limited. It Cannot Silence Courage"**

I have a special favor to ask of everyone that is part of my support team. I have an extraordinary and dear friend of mine, who is a recent cancer survivor. Unfortunately, I was just informed that the doctors have discovered that cancer has returned, and she is beginning a radiation treatment program as I write this email. I know many of you have prayer groups and prayer chains, and I would appreciate it if you would please include my friend Judy in your prayers. She is an exceptional and dear person, and I want to have many more luncheons with her. I want to thank you in advance for your prayers and support.

Just like me, *Cathy's Corner* will be taking a little rest for a few weeks. I will update everyone as I start my next treatment phase, around the 9th of October.

So I will sign off with three songs to keep you humming and a few photos to keep you smiling.

This week's songs:

"Celebrate Me Home"...Kenny Loggins—this song was recommended by our friend Rhonda from Orange County, CA.

"Footloose"...Kenny Loggins—our upbeat song of the week

"Be Good to Yourself"...Journey

This week's photos are from my birthday; I am showing the photo of my special orange birthday cupcakes. Notice my new wig. I have included a photo of me and my middle son, Bob, that shows what my real hair looked like before Mr. Luekemia came into my life.

5.

By the third month, Cathy was completely hairless everywhere on her body. Now the thought of not needing to shave her legs was refreshing; however, being bald was still tough to get used to. Being that her hair was down to the middle of her back most of her life and was close to shoulder length at the time she became sick, made the total loss of hair a large pill to swallow. She had purchased two wigs that very closely resembled her shoulder-length hair but found them too hot to wear, especially in Florida. She did wear them occasionally but found that her bling hats and the vast selection of scarves that were given to her by family and friends were comfortable and yet stylish.

For the next four months, Cathy and Joe repeated the treatment process between home and the hospital with a few hiccups and side effects but nothing major. She did not have the sickness or vomiting side effects that some chemo patients have. However, she did have the weakness and extreme tiredness, causing her to spend most of her time at home resting, her body struggling to bring back strength to endure another round of treatment. One time her doctor went on vacation, and the doctor that was filling in for her commented to Dr. Lukeman that she was giving Cathy a powerful and aggressive formula of chemo in which Dr. Lukeman replied: "I know, I want her to beat this monster and get better."

There were some bright spots during her months of treatment. There was a time her youngest son from Georgia and his wife came down to visit, and, on their way home, they stopped and donated blood in Cathy's name. This was greatly appreciated, during her treatment there were periods that Cathy's blood and platelets would become low and they would have to give her blood or platelets to get her body up to an acceptable level. The next week it so happened that Cathy needed to be given some blood and believe it or not; she was given the blood of her youngest son, Jaison that was donated the prior week. When you are given blood, the bag of blood has the name of the donor and Cathy always checked the name because she knew there were people from work, family members, friends and even a few of the nurses that were caring for her were donating blood on an ongoing basis in her name. Another time she received the blood of her nurse as well as a few people from her work.

The support team continued to be the bright spot of Cathy's fight. They would text her after reading the latest Cathy's Corner and tell her how proud they were of her, how she inspired them with her tenacity to beat this vicious monster. Some would email her thoughts and prayers, and there were a few that sent her a get-well card every week, rain or shine, to let her know that they were fighting this battle with her. "Nobody Fights Alone." Cathy would always say with tears in her eyes that she was going to win her fight because she was determined not to let her friends and family down. Perhaps it was that spirit that the support team created for her that became the significant plus factor in helping her get through the lows of fighting cancer.

The remaining months of Cathy's Corner have been made available for publication. The next five months of Cathy's treatments are on the following pages.

Cathy's Corner "No One Fights Alone" 10-8-2013
Back in the saddle again... Ready to start climbing mountain #4.

Well... as you can see, I am back in the hospital and beginning my fourth month of chemo treatment. The check-in went smoothly, and I was in my room by 7:00 p.m. last night. The rest at home was great, and it seemed that the time flew by so fast. I honestly was not ready to come back, but what's a girl going to do? I went to the doctors last Wednesday for my regular blood check-up, and my hemoglobin count was down, which meant that I had to come into the hospital (as an outpatient) on Friday and have two bags of blood administered. Six hours later, I was as good as Count Dracula after a night at a Transylvania Festival. **Hey!!!!! it is October and Halloween is not far off.** As always, I am waiting to see how I respond to this treatment even though I had this treatment before and handled it well. I was exhausted this time when I was at home, and the doctor told me that this is normal due to the fact that I just had three months of chemo treatments and that my body was feeling the effects.

It was so lovely to get some good home cooking; I was getting tired of the hospital food, and it's bland taste. Joe did a new bowtie pasta dish with a four-cheese sauce with shrimp. Now you have that pasta dish and a loaf of Publix's fresh-baked Italian bread, and you have yourself a meal that is **"DAGGUM GOOD"** (as they say in the south). You also have no idea how good fresh mashed potato's taste after seventeen days in the hospital.

Some of you are coming close to the date that you can donate blood again and have asked if I still needed blood donations. Yes, I usually have anywhere from four to six bags of blood given to me each stay in the hospital. You can go into any One Blood Center and inform them that you wish to donate blood for a specific person. Inform them you are donating for Cathy Acct # 305587 (if you don't have or remember the account # you can still give, but they will have to look up all of the information.) also keep in mind that the blood keeps well and should last a few months. I appreciate the donations, and I thank you in advance for your contribution.

I will update you by the weekend on how everything is progressing.

Cathy's comment of the day:
What cancer cannot do—**"Cancer is so limited, it cannot reduce eternal life."**

Our Triple Tuesday song selections are:
"Cherry Bomb"...John Cougar Mellencamp; this is a special request for Chuck, Cathy's Coworker

"We're an American Band"...Grand Funk Railroad, upbeat song of the day

"Twilight Zone"...Golden Earring

Keeping the Prayers On High Beam
Love & Prayers
Ms. Cathy

Cathy's Corner "Nobody Fights Alone" 10-14-2013
Turning the Corner on Treatment # 4

The Chemo for treatment phase # 4 has been completed, YEA!!!!!!!!!!!!!!!!!!!!!!!!!!!!!! All I have to do now is have my Intrathecal (Chemo shot into the spine) on Wednesday. Then it is build up and go home.

I hope that I can be out of here no later than next Tuesday (hopefully earlier) as Joe and I will be celebrating our 42nd wedding anniversary next Wednesday, October 23. We will do Cathy's Corner next week with specially dedicated love songs.

This round has gone pretty well so far. Side effects have been minimum, with tiredness being the most common. The good news is that they drew some spinal fluid during the last intrathecal to check to see if there were any cancer cells, and so far, everything looks clean and clear. I am still bald, and what new hair started to grow has already fallen out.

I got a new wig before I came into the hospital, and my hairdresser Shari came over to trim and fix it for me. It is a little lighter than my hair was, and I even think they threw in a few gray hairs (no charge). I will attach a picture of me and my son Bob; my wig looks just like my hair in the photo.

You know the beautiful thing about October is that the color orange is a primary color for the month. From pumpkins, fall leaves, Halloween decorations, to scary Jack-O-Lanterns, the color orange is all around us. So let's all pick a lovely fall day and wear something orange for both Halloween and leukemia.

I know that this Cathy's Corner will be short and sweet, but I want you all to know that a day does not go by that I do not thank the Lord for my friends and family. I know that the prayers are always going strong, and I know that I am just a few months away from winning this battle. So remember as you think and pray for me, I am praying and giving thanks for your love and friendship.

Cathy's Comment of the Day: What Cancer Cannot Do— **"CANCER IS SO LIMITED, it cannot quench the Spirit"**

Today's Songs Selections are:

The Power of Prayers: Jesus is Just Alright...The Doobie Brothers

To Mr. Leukemia: "Don't Bring Me·Down"...E.L.O.

To my Support Team: "You Have a Friend"...James Taylor

"Dixie Hoedown"...Nitty Gritty Dirt Band
(Remember to tap your feet.)

Today I am including two photos of why life is so important to me—my sons as little boys and then as young men. My life would not be complete without them.

Keeping the Prayers on High Beam
Love and Prayers
Ms. Cathy

Cathy's Corner "No One Fights Alone" 10-23-2013
Going Home......................Finally

Believe it or not, I am finally going home tonight, just in time for my anniversary. It was a close call timewise. I had completed all of my chemo treatments, my intrathecal, and started my Neupogen shots to increase my white blood cells and wouldn't you know it, I ended up with a fever and a slight infection around my port. Just as things were looking great... **BAM!**

The infectious disease doctors were in my room immediately and started administering all kinds of antibiotics. I think I had three different medicines going at the same time. It was like the hazmat team from *E. T.* Anyway, they did an excellent job, and it appears that it was a mild infection, and it is under control. So now my white blood cell count is up, and I get to go home BUT!!!!!!!!!!!! not before they give me two pints of blood to get my hemoglobin count up before I leave. First, I needed the hospitalist to release me, then the oncologist to release me, then the infectious disease doctor to release me. Once everyone signed off, and I receive my two pints, I am a free woman. Sometimes I think it easier to get an early release from prison than it is to gain discharge from the hospital. (My Florida friends will get the humor there.)

Now my new blood. As I said above, I needed to have two pints of blood administered before I leave, so when they brought me my first bag of blood, I noticed the pink card on the bag shows who donated in your name. I looked at the tag and it was given by the son of one my good friends Michele Brown...**NOW HOW COOL IS THAT?**

Then when they bought the second bag of blood, I looked at the pink tag, and the blood was from Michele Brown's husband...**NOW, HOW COOL IS THAT? An extraordinary thanks to the Brown family you guys are GREAT.**

If everything goes to plan, I should be home until sometime around November 7. I am so looking forward to being home and the freedom of going out and doing stuff. As I said at the beginning of Cathy's Corner, tomorrow (October 23), Joe and I will be celebrating our 42nd wedding anniversary. Can you believe it's been forty-two years, three loving sons, three special and loving daughters-in-law, and two wonderful, beautiful grandchildren later, and it still feels like it all was just a few years ago? We plan on spending some quiet time together (that is the phrase you use when you get older instead of saying making whoopee) and plan on going to Mt. Dora for their annual craft show with Joe Jr. and his wife, Andrea.

We are looking forward to making the 50th-anniversary mark when we plan on having a significant celebration. I already have a dance reserved with my grandson. (He should be around ten years old by then.)

Therefore today's songs are dedicated to our anniversary.

To Cathy & Joe: "Gimme Some Lovin'"...Spencer Davis Group

Joe to Cathy: "Forever's as Far as I'll Go"...Alabama

Cathy to Joe: Since I could not come up with one song to dedicate to Joe, I decided to write this note of dedication to him. "Betcha by Golly Wow" after 42 years, I know our love is here to stay. Joe, you are "My First, My Last, My Everything," as well as "My Guy." "Only you," Joe, have "My Endless Love" as I "Only Have Eyes for You." "I Will Always Love You," "Always and Forever."

Today's Photo ....from Joe

This photo is of Cathy. As you know, last month we celebrated Cathy's birthday, and some of you wanted to know how old she was. Well, I am not at liberty to say. Still, I have attached a photo of Cathy and General Robert E Lee @ Gettysburg, PA. (You do the math)

Happy Halloween to everyone!!!!!!!!!!!!
Keeping the Prayers on High Beam
Love and Prayers
Ms. Cathy

Cathy's Corner "No One Fights Alone" 10-31-2013
Climbing Mountain # 5........... But with a revised plan of action

Well... I am back at my favorite Hospital Inn. I checked in yesterday and began preparing for climbing mountain #5. This month's treatment is the aggressive chemo phase that knocks you out. The good thing is that I do not have to do any more injections into the spine, so this will be a little better than the past treatments. I went to see my oncologist for checkups when I was home, and all of the bloodwork came back good. I was maintaining proper levels of platelets, hemoglobin, and white blood cells. However, we discussed the chemo treatments and the time table. Even though my oncologist is happy with my progress and the way I am handling the procedures, she still has our goal set on complete remission vs. partial remission. Of course, for us to accomplish complete remission, we would have to do eight treatments vs. the six treatments I was hoping for. My type of leukemia regimen calls for eight treatments of chemo before doing the bone marrow analysis. In some cases, patients have stopped chemo after six treatments; however, the chance of a reoccurrence is more significant than if you completed all eight chemo treatments. After some discussion, we agreed that we had come too far to stop at six treatments. SO... I will be getting the full eight treatments, which means the chemo will be completed by late February, provided that there are no setbacks. Trust me, no one was more disappointed than me, but I do not want to go through this again. I want this to a one-time experience. I was so looking forward to going back to work with my friends and making a few trips to Atlanta to see my precious grandchildren, but everyone will have to be a little more patient and keep those Prayers on High Beam just a little longer.

My time at home was excellent. Our anniversary was very nice. We did not do anything special, just a little R&R, but we were together without any hospital staff checking upon us. We went to the craft fair in Mt. Dora with our son Joe and his wife, Andrea. The best part of the fair was that I was able to see and spend time with some of my friends from work. It was one of the most beautiful days while I was at home.

Joe and I went to the movies to see *Last Vegas*, the film with Robert De Niro, Michael Douglas, Morgan Freeman, and Kevin Kline. It was one of the funniest movies I had seen in a long time. If you are under sixty, it is hilarious but, if sixty and over, it is a riot!!!!!!!!!!!!!!!!!!!!!!!!! I laughed so hard I had tears running down my face. If you get a chance and want to see a fun movie and laugh, I would recommend this one.

Cathy's comment of the day: "Just know, when you truly want success, you will never give up on it. No matter how bad the situation may get."

Today's Song Selections:

We added two new friends from West Virginia to Cathy's Corner, so the first song is dedicated to them. We are going to keep this week's songs upbeat.

"Thank God I'm a Country Boy"...John Denver

"Free Bird (Live)"...Lynyrd Skynyrd

"Orange Blossom Special"...Flying Burrito Brothers

Until the next update.............................
Keeping the Prayers on High Beam
Love & Prayers
Ms. Cathy

Cathy's Corner "No One Fights alone" 12-4-2013
Here We Go Again.......Treatment # 6 is underway

Wow, where did the time go? It seems like I just left this place. Isn't it funny how fast time goes when you are home and how slow time goes when you are in the hospital? Even though time seemed to fly by, I had a delightful time at home. The side effects and tiredness last longer after each treatment, which means more rest is needed to build yourself back up for the next procedure. Each treatment kills everything in your blood as it tries to convince your body to quit making cancer cells. The only problem is that it wears your body down over a period of time. I guess it could be compared to a boxer in a boxing match that keeps getting knocked down, the first time the fighter gets knocked down, he jumps up and gets back into the fight, however, after he gets knocked down six or seven times, he starts to get back up a little slower each time. But, with perseverance and determination, he ends up winning the boxing match and is crowned the victor. So, all I have to do is **"Fight Like a Woman"** and get back up three more times, and I will be beat this monster. Somehow I see this more as a motivation/inspiration than a hindrance. In **_My Heart_**, I know I am winning.

I hope each of you had a happy and enjoyable Thanksgiving. My Thanksgiving turned out to be fabulous. Jaison and his wife made the trip down from Atlanta with my two beautiful grandchildren. We also had Joe Jr., and Jaison's in-laws to make it an exceptional day for all of us. The food was great, the company was extraordinary, and the time together was precious. I could not have asked for a better day. Our Georgia Peach is growing so fast and is the cutest five-month-old little girl. (of course, I am partial) She loved sleeping in Grandma's arms. Our grandson has grown into quite a little man. He has the cutest laugh and has more energy than the Energizer Bunny and loves going outdoors as much as possible. He picked up all of our pinecones, sticks, and fallen grapefruit out of the backyard and, with the help of Uncle Joe, tossed them over the fence. (no… not in our neighbor's yard, in the ditch behind the house.)

And… The best news is they are coming back after Christmas Day and staying until Jan 1. Joe and I are so excited; we have a lot of activities and fun planned. **AND** to make it the best **Christmas ever**… our son Bob and his wife, Megan are coming down from Pittsburgh. So we will have all three boys, their wives, and our grandchildren together. I will have a lot of pictures to share when I come back in January.

Cathy's Comment.................What Cancer Cannot Do.............. Cancer is so limited it cannot take away your humanity or your compassion…**From my friend Trish**

This Editions Songs (of course we are going with Christmas Songs)

"I'll be home for Christmas"…Carly Simon (Cathy's pick)

Our upbeat song picks

"Wizards in Winter"…TSO

"Mad Russian's Christmas"…TSO

"Wish Liszt"…TSO

Joe and I have attended TSO's annual concert for six years, and every year the concert is better than the previous year. An amazing group of artists. I would recommend that you see them perform if you ever get the chance.

Until the next edition..............
KEEPING THE PRAYERS ON HIGH BEAM
Ms. Cathy

Cathy's Corner "No One Fights Alone" 12-19-2013

HOORAY!!!!!!!!!!!!!!!! Treatment # 6 is in the history books. Now it's time for Christmas, the Grandkids, and the start of a shiny and promising New Year.

This round of chemo went well. It took longer for me to build back up than it did to have the chemo treatments. We are down to two more months of chemo treatment, then the test to confirm remission. Let's all keep our fingers crossed and prayers strong as we come down to the final stretch. The next procedure will be the last of the real aggressive type (the one that knocks me on my butt), so I am going to make the **best** of the Christmas holidays and the time with my sons, daughters-in-law, and grandkids before I head back to kick Mr. Leukemia's butt. I am still fighting the constant fatigue, but the adrenaline of the holidays and my grandchildren are keeping my spirits high.

Now for a good-hearted story. During my recent stay, I was given three bags of blood and two bags of platelets. This was expected; however, what makes it heartwarming is that during my November hospital stay, one of my nurses (**Arlene**) had decided to donate blood in my name. Many of my friends and family have donated blood for me (which I am forever grateful). However, when you think of how many cancer patients there are at the hospital, it is apparent that I was blessed to have Arlene care enough that she would donate blood in my name. Now, what makes it even more special is the day that I received my first bag of blood, guess where the blood came from????? and guess who my nurse was that gave it to me??????? You got it ....**Arlene**

NOW, HOW COOL IS THAT!!!!!!!!!!!!!!!! (she did go out and buy a lottery ticket after that, and she did win a dollar (a real trifecta))

Joe and I are excited to have the kids home for the holidays and plan on making this an extraordinary holiday season.

Jaison's family will show up on December 27, and Bob and Megan are coming down from "The Burgh" on the 30th, and of course, Joe Jr. and his wife live in Apopka, so we will see them on Christmas Day and throughout the week. We plan on taking a lot of photos, so get ready to see some updated pictures when I do the next edition of Cathy's Corner.

As I prepare for this Christmas season, I want all of you (yens-Pittsburghese, You'll or you all- the south) to know how blessed I am to have each of you as part of my family. Your emails, texts, cards continue to be the motivation that keeps me on a positive path of success in beating this monster. I want to wish every one of you a **VERY MERRY CHRISTMAS and A Prosperous NEW YEAR. May the magic of the Christmas Season be in your hearts all year.**

Cathy's Comment: "It's not without fear; it's having the determination to go on in spite of it."

This editions song recommendation:

To my support team: "You Make Me So Very Happy"...Blood, Sweat, and Tears, from our friend John Lattimore

My Holiday Selection

"Home for the Holidays"...Perry Como (he is from Pittsburgh. He was a barber before his singing career)

"Silent Night"...Susan Boyle

"Hark! The Herald Angels Sing"...Christmas Joy CD

Until January 2014
Merry Christmas

"Keeping The Prayers on High Beam"
Love & Prayers
Ms. Cathy

6.

It was during her hospital stay for her seventh month of chemo treatment that Cathy received the news that she had been waiting to hear since her treatments had started. Dr. Lukeman had just walked into her hospital room and smiled as she apprised Cathy that the recent three blood test results have indicated that her body was no longer creating cancer cells. It appears that she is in remission and cancer free for the first time since July 2013.

Needless to say, Cathy started crying. Dr. Lukeman smiled and stated, "Why are you crying? I thought you would be happy," to which Cathy responded, saying, "I am happy, words cannot explain how happy I am. What you see are 'Tears of Joy,' for I have waited seven long months for you to tell you that I am cancer free. Once Cathy composed herself, she called Joe to break the great news to him as they both shared "Tears of Joy" over the phone.

Dr. Lukeman explained to Cathy that they would continue her current treatment as well as have her come back in two weeks to complete the eighth and final month of treatment, at which time they would do a bone marrow biopsy to confirm the state of her remission.

That evening Cathy and her husband celebrated her great news as they talked about all of the things that they were going to do together, such as trips to Georgia to see their grandchildren, trips to their camp in PA., and their European Viking cruise they were going to take to celebrate their 50th wedding anniversary, as Cathy started her journey back to a healthy life once again. They decided that they would wait until next month's publication of Cathy's Corner to break the news to the support team. However, tonight was their night, and they were going to make it as special as possible.

Unfortunately, neither one of them was aware at the time that the celebration would be short-lived as they would learn in a few weeks that the monster was merely hiding and regrouping as it was planning another attack.

Cathy's Corner "No One Fights Alone" 1-7-2014
HAPPY NEW YEAR!!!! To all of my friends and family. 2014 is going to be my year to shine.

Now that the holidays are behind me, the grandkids had gone home more spoiled than when they came, and my sons and daughters-in-law have returned to the everyday grind of the real world, it is time to start treatment # 7 (of 8). I went back to the hospital on Monday, Jan 6, and chemo started today. The good news is that this is the last one of the aggressive chemo treatments. As you know from past editions of Cathy's Corners this is the one that hits hard, and the recovery is always slow and tough but, this is the last one. **YEA!!!!!!!!!!!!!!!!!!**

It is such a good feeling to know that I am getting closer to the end of my treatment program. It is still hard to believe that I have been at it for seven months and when I complete this month I will only have one month of chemo left, **DOUBLE YEA!!!!!!!!!!!!!!!!!!!!!!!!!!!!!!!!!** I guess you can say that the light at the end of the tunnel is getting brighter every day.

I did learn today that the plan of action after treatment #8 is a two to three-week break then I come back to the hospital for the bone marrow procedure. The doctors inject a long needle into the hip bone and draw out the bone marrow and check to make sure it is no longer producing cancerous cells. If everything checks out good, I will officially be in remission. Then I will have to get my blood checked monthly (probably for the rest of my life). Statistics have shown that a leukemia survivor that stays in remission for at least five years has an excellent chance of staying cancer free.

Now that we have the medical update over with we can now talk about my fabulous "Home for the Holidays."

Well, it turned out to be the best Christmas and New Year gift a mother could receive. We started by spending Christmas Eve at our neighbor's open house with good food and good friends. Then at Christmas, we spent the day with Joe Jr. and his wife. On the 26th Jaison and his family from Atlanta arrived, followed by Bob and Megan coming on the 30th. Now our holidays were complete. The time spent with the grandkids was by far the most fun we had since Daddy took the T-Bird away. (lyrics from Beach Boys song) The grandchildren are the most excellent Christmas present a grandma could receive even if it were for only a few days. The time went fast, but the love, laughs, and hugs will be my heart forever. Having all three boys, their wives, and the grandkids home was a dream come true.

Cathy's Comment:
In overcoming any challenge, the essential factor is "believing you can win." Without believing, there can be no successful outcome.

Song Selection:
Since it is a new year, we are going to start with a very upbeat, swing tempo but first a Beatle favorite.

"The Long and Winding Road"...The Beatles

Now let's get in the swing mood
"Boogie Bumper"...Big Bad Voodoo Daddy

"Mambo Swing"...Big Bad Voodoo Daddy

"Jumpin' Jack"...Big Bad Voodoo Daddy

Until our next edition
Keeping the prayers on High Beam
Love & Prayers
Ms. Cathy

Cathy's Corner "No One Fights Alone" 1-25-2014
Treatment #7 is in the History Books......... Now
at home, resting and preparing for treatment #8.

Treatment # 7 was tough and aggressive, but I handled it well, considering everything. It seemed to take a little longer to get my strength back to where I could go home, but I am home now and enjoying the chilly January weather. My hair is showing signs of growing again, and I hope that it keeps growing. Well, I have only one more treatment of chemo left. I should return around February 3rd to start the 8th and final treatment of chemo(let's hope and pray that it is the final one) then I will have the bone marrow extraction to see if the bone marrow is cancer free and not producing cancer cells. I know that I have said it before, but words cannot express my feelings of appreciation and gratitude for the amount of love and support everyone continues to show me during this long and winding road of treatment. The continuous e-mails, texts, cards, and prayers fill my days with happiness and determination to win this battle. You have no idea how eight months of chemo treatment and hospital stays can wear down a person's mind and soul; it gets old fast. But because of you, I am able to keep everything in perspective and stay healthy. My success will be a result of the support, love, and prayers from everyone, and I anxiously await for the victory of beating this monster. The end is close, and the light at the end of the tunnel is getting brighter.

Now for a good-hearted story...................... When Jaison and his wife were at our home for Christmas, they went to One Blood and donated platelets and blood in my name. During my recent stay in the hospital, I had to have platelets and blood infusion. Well................. when they brought in the Blood into my room it had a pink tag (which designates that it was given in my name) and guess what.............. YOU GOT IT........... It was my daughter in law's blood that I received **NOW HOW COOL IS THAT** !!!!!!!!!!!!!!!!!!!!! It is moments like this that you do feel the **love** and **caring** that everyone continues to give me during this battle.

Now that I am home, the first thing on my list is to make a huge pot of homemade chicken noodle soup...................... Now that is "DAGGUM GOOD" Soup. Those little Campbell Kids have nothing on me

Cathy's Comment: Remember that after the end of every day. There is a new tomorrow full of exciting new things.

This edition's song selections are:

"Gonna Have a Party"...Alabama (Super Bowl Sunday song)

"Gimme Shelter"...Grand Funk Railroad (Upbeat Song)

To my support Team: "How Sweet It Is (to be Loved by You)" ... James Taylor

Until the next edition of Cathy's Corner...
Keep Warm and Smile often

"Keeping the Prayers on High Beam"
Love and Prayers
Ms. Cathy

Cathy's Corner, "No One Fights Alone." 2-5-2014

OK Baby, Open the gate.................... I am back for # eight................ Can you believe it!!!!!!

Back at Florida Hospital for (hopefully) my last treatment of chemo. There has been a slight delay in the treatment cycle due to my white blood cells being too low even though I had three Neupogen shots during my homestay. So I will get a Neupogen shot to build up the white cells as well as work on increasing my PH. I should hopefully start chemo Thursday. I guess after seven months of chemo, it just takes a little longer for my body to recover from my last treatment. So I will keep the chin up and stay positive.

My stay at home was pleasant and restful. I was able to enjoy the cool weather and spend time with my neighbors and friends. I finally took down the Christmas tree. Thankfully it is an artificial tree. Of course, the time went by so fast, and it seemed like I just got home, and it was time to come back.

One of the beautiful things that happened to me when I was home was my neighbor and friend Joanna came to visit and gave me a book that was written by her sister. It is titled Nature Speaks Written by Melanie Wade. It is a beautiful book about the wonders of my Father's world. It is filled with stories about the wonders of our world that surround us, along with beautiful scriptures quotes. Thank you, Joanna, I appreciate your gift.

Then Joe and I went over to our other neighbor's house for the first half of the Super Bowl and had some excellent ribs, beans, snacks, and drinks (nonalcohol for me). The food was excellent, and the game was so-so. I only get excited about Super Bowls when the Steelers are playing.

Cathy's Comment:
Believe with all of your heart that you will do what you were made to do.

Today's song selections have a special message:

To Mr. Leukemia: "I am Woman"...Helen Reddy

To Mr. Leukemia: "I Won't Back Down"...Tom Petty

To my support team: "You Light Up My Life"–...
Debbie Boone

Keeping the Prayers on High Beam
Love & Prayers
Ms. Cathy

Cathy's Corner "No One Fights Alone" 2-23-2014
The Journey Comes To An End...I am finally home... YEA!! YEA!!

The eight months of a long and winding road has finally come to an end. It took a little longer than I wanted for my white blood cells count to get up to where I could go home, but they finally kicked in, and I checked out of Hotel Florida Hospital on Saturday Morning. I had a strange feeling leaving the hospital this time, definitely mixed emotions. For the past seven months, when I left the hospital, I always knew that I was coming back, but not this time. I am in **remission**, and I have canceled all future reservations at Hotel Florida Hospital. On the other hand, I have come to know and appreciate a very gifted, professional, and exclusive group of Nurses, Techs, and Doctors that helped me win my battle. Many of them I now consider my friends as they have been a crucial part of my support team. Now that I am home, it is time to start to build up my body's immune system and work on getting back to a healthy lifestyle. **HOORAY!!!!!!!!!!!!!!!!!!!!!!!!**

I have received texts, e-mails, and phone calls after my last Cathy's Corner announcing my **REMISSION,** and I thank all of you from the bottom of my heart. I know I have said it over and over for the past eight months, but I meant it when I said that you were a crucial part of me winning my battle with Leukemia. Everyone has been part of the best support team that any cancer patient that goes into battle could ask for. Your love, prayers, texts, and cards were the fuel that kept me fighting day after day.

To My Support Team I leave you with the following:

When my spirits were high, you were there to keep me smiling, dancing to some good music, and share the good times.

When my spirits were low, you somehow knew that I needed you, and you sent cards, texts, and emails that quickly turned my frown into a smile.

When I silently prayed, I always felt that I could hear your prayers along with mine.

Words cannot express my feelings and gratitude, so all I can say is **THANK YOU, YOU ARE A SPECIAL PERSON, and I AM HONORED TO HAVE YOU AS MY FRIEND.**

Cathy's Comment:
We are all strangers to our hidden potential until we confront problems that reveal our true capabilities.

Our song selection:
over the past eight months, we have selected over forty-five songs that inspired us, let us boogie to Charlie Daniels, Alabama, Grand Funk Railroad, and Lynyrd Skynyrd, brought in the holidays, challenged Mr. Leukemia, and expressed our love to our friends and family.

Therefore, it is only appropriate that the last song of Cathy's Corner will be dedicated to all current and future cancer patients. May it give them the hope and courage to beat this monster.

"You'll Never Walk Alone"...IL DIVO

In closing, I will do an update soon on my progress, but for the most part, Cathy's Corner "No One Fights Alone" has just published it's "FINAL EDITION."

"KEEPING THE PRAYERS ON HIGH BEAM"
Love & Prayers
Ms. Cathy

"A NEW JOURNEY BEGINS"
7.

The eighth month of treatment started with pure excitement and jubilation. The final month of chemo was to begin, and life would slowly return to the good ol' days. As Cathy was receiving her treatment, the medical team performed the final bone marrow biopsy for an examination that included the Bone Marrow Transplant team of Florida Hospital. As the Bone Marrow Transplant team reviewed the biopsy report, they discovered a problem that had not shown up in previous reports. It appeared that Cathy had lost a set of numbers in her DNA. Everyone has ten sets of numbers that repeat themselves throughout their DNA, and Cathy only had nine sets of numbers repeating throughout her DNA. It was apparent she had dropped a set of numbers in her DNA. The medical team did not know if the disappearance of her numbers happened before, which could have initially caused the leukemia, or did the set of numbers evaporate during the chemo treatments. The one clear thing was the fact she was missing a set of numbers, and the result was that the Leukemia was destined to return. The medical team had no idea when it would happen, it could be three weeks, three months, or three years but the odds were very high that it would show its ugly face again. The other fact that was apparent was the odds of Cathy's body and organs handling an aggressive chemo treatment like she just went through a second time were not in her favor.

The medical team went into Cathy's hospital room and discussed with her their findings. They explained to her that she had two options; Option 1 was to wait and see how long it will take for the leukemia to return, and Option 2 was to consider having a stem cell transplant. However, a stem cell transplant involved a few different facets before it can happen. The most crucial piece of the puzzle was to find a donor that matched at least eight sets of numbers of her DNA, then have the donor give consent to donating their stem cells to Cathy. The next step would prepare her body to receive the stem cells, and after 100 days of quarantine to verify if her body accepted the stem cells. Which if they did, she can begin the five-year treatment process to monitor her progress in case her body suddenly decided to reject the new stem cells. If she can stay healthy and continue to make the new stem cells, the odds of her Leukemia returning would be less than 10% at the end of the five years.

Cathy immediately phoned Joe and broke the news to him of the recent findings and the options on the table. As they talked, she explained that she was so disappointed and overwhelmed by the news of the day. Cathy needed to know what his thoughts were on the situation. At which time he said to her that he was as disappointed as much as she was, however, "It is what it is" and being upset was not going to help the situation. They needed to focus on the new challenge in front of them and meet that challenge head-on with the same positive attitude they used with her leukemia. He told her that in his mind, it was a no brainer. She would never find the happiness she was looking for if she spent the days, months, or years looking over her shoulder to see if the monster is hiding in the shadows. She would never have a decent night's sleep or peace of mind the rest of the days ahead. In his opinion, the only solution was the stem cell transplant with the hopes that they could find a donor before the monster returns. Cathy agreed as she knew all along that the stem cell transplant was the answer; she just needed her husband to confirm her feelings. He told her that he would be at the hospital soon, and they can meet with the medical team and create a strategy with a plan of action.

After arriving at the hospital and meeting with the medical team to discuss the next steps, Cathy and her husband retreated to the hospital room to debrief in private what just happened. The one thing they did agree on was that Cathy needed to complete this treatment cycle, and they would hope and pray that the next challenge would be as smooth as the Chemo treatment. What they didn't know was that they were venturing into a different world that made eight months of chemo look like a walk in the park.

During the last week of Cathy's treatment, she had a thank-you luncheon for all of the nurses, supervisors, and medical doctors that were around. She wanted to show her appreciation for everything they had done for the past eight months. It was two luncheons one during the day for the day team and one that evening for the night team. She had met an elite group of doctors, and made good friends with most of the nurses during her eight months stay at "Hotel Florida Hospital."

Cathy and Joe decided to keep the stem cell situation under wraps, except for the immediate family, from the support team until they had more accurate information with dates and times.

On the last day of Cathy's hospital day, they published the final edition of Cathy's Corner with a promise of occasion updates from time to time. They knew from the past months' many people would patiently wait for the next edition of Cathy's Corner and when they did not receive it in the time frame, they thought it should have been sent, they would send Cathy text messages or emails asking when the next edition was coming. They were by far the best support team a person could ever hope to have.

Cathy and her husband left the hospital happy as they anxiously waited for the next phone call to happen.

Cathy's Corner – "A New Journey" Begins 3-24-2014
Hello Everyone. HAPPY SPRING!!!!!!!!!!!!!!!!!!!!!!
Don't you just love that extra hour of daylight?????

It has been a few weeks since our last publication of Cathy's Corner, and I wanted to bring everyone up to date on what is happening in my life and state of recovery.

The good news is I am feeling great, and my hair is starting to grow back. However, in spite of my complete remission, I have learned that I have to undertake "A New Journey" to ensure that the Leukemia does not come back. During the doctor's analysis of the bone marrow biopsy, it became apparent that my DNA only had a set of nine numbers instead of the standard set of ten numbers. Somehow my DNA dropped a set of numbers, and the medical team had no idea how or when my DNA changed. This change in my DNA means that it is classified as aggressive and in a radical state. This discovery implies that the Leukemia will return. The doctors don't know what the timetable would be, but it is highly probable it will return. I have two options; the first is to do nothing and wait and see how long before Leukemia returns or have a stem cell transplant with hopes of creating new DNA. Considering that if leukemia did return, my petite five-foot body would be able to handle another eight months of chemo. The chances of the chemo destroying my internal organs would be high. Therefore, I have decided to opt for a stem cell transplant.

I am currently scheduled to have a Stem Cell Transplant April 1st to hopefully get my body to create a new immune system that will prevent the return of the monster leukemia. I know everyone has a ton of questions, so I think the best way to address what is happening is through a

Q&A format
Q. Why a stem cell transplant, you are in complete remission???

A. Yes, I am in complete remission; however, my DNA is damaged, and there is a high percentage (70%), and the chances of Leukemia returning increases as the months/years pass by. The reason I developed leukemia in the first place was due to a breakdown in my DNA, which in turn started creating cancer cells. My immune system was not able to repair the DNA or fight off the cancer cells as they began to multiply in my body. When this occurs, your immune system becomes tolerant of the cancer cells in your blood, and over time we all know what the outcome is. The ultimate goal through the eight months of chemo is to kill all of the cancer cells and have the DNA repair itself and become what they call rested.

Well, I accomplished the first phase, and the cancer cells are eliminated, and my DNA stopped producing cancer cells, but it did not repair itself and have not achieved a state of normalcy. When this happens, you have two options:

1. You go through life looking over your shoulder, wondering when Mr. Leukemia is going to show his ugly face, knowing that when he does, you more than likely will not be able to handle another eight months of chemo. But then who knows, maybe he will never come back (chances are 15 to 20 percent he might not come back).

2. You see, if you qualify as a stem cell transplant candidate and hope that they find a match that enables you to have a stem cell transplant.

As you know, I am not much of a gambler, and I do not want to spend my future worrying and looking over my back, so I have decided to move forward with the Stem Cell Transplant.

Q. You said find a match. Have they found a match? And how did they find your match?

A. Yes, I am blessed. The transplant team has found me a match; my donor is a twenty-year-old male and lives in the USA. The process of finding a match is a very detailed, delicate, thorough procedure. The medical team takes your DNA and sends it to Marrow and Cord Blood transplant center named "BE THE MATCH." They have a database of approximately Ten million potential donors for a stem cell or bone marrow transplant. They then begin the search for a donor that matches the ten key numbers of my DNA. It took about a month, and they found a 9 out of 10 point match. I cannot have a ten out of ten as the damaged part of my DNA has lost its number sequence.

Q. How do they get the stem cells?

A. The medical team pulls the donor's blood through a machine that separates the Stem Cells from the blood and then returns the blood to his body. They will preserve the stem cells and ship overnight the stem cells to the hospital. The stem cells will then be transplanted via I.V. into my bloodstream.

Q. Do you have to have chemo again?

A. Yes, I'm afraid so. I go into the hospital on Tuesday, March 25. They will begin Chemo on Wednesday, and I will have four days of chemo to kill my immune system and bone marrow. I will have two days' rest, and the Stem Transplant will commence on April 1. April 1 will be my new birthday as the new Cathy will be born.

Q. How does the Stem Cell Transplant prevent the Leukemia from coming back.

A. I will explain in detail the grafting process in the next publication, but the Readers Digest version is that as the months/years pass by, the chances increase that it will not return. Just the opposite of the above scenario.

Q. What is your recovery timetable??

A. The total recovery depends on how well my body handles and reacts to the transplant. The first 100 days are the most critical. I will be in the hospital for at least thirty days, and when I am released to go home, I will not be permitted to go outside or be around groups of people. I will go back for checkups three times a week until I reach a point that I do not need to go back as often. I will be on a strict neutropenic diet and will not be allowed fresh fruits and vegetables. Everything will need to be cooked well done. I will not have an immune system for a while. Therefore, I will be in a special room in the hospital that has its own air filtration system. The door to my hospital room has to remain closed at all times, and anyone that comes into my room must wear a mask and wash their hands a zillion times. (Well maybe not a zillion but more than usual)

Q. What hospital will this transplant take place.?
A. Florida Hospital South, Rollins Ave, Orlando

If you would like to learn more about the transplant process feel free to go to ***BeTheMatch.org***

I guess I have given everyone enough info to get a good understanding of what is happening in my life.

So once again, I am reaching out to you, my special friends and loved ones (my support team) to join me once again in praying for a successful transplant. We are praying for successful grafting of my donor's stem cells to my bone marrow and that I do not encounter any infections or viruses during this highly critical time of healing.

Cathy's Comment: I have found that if you love life, life will love you back. (Arthur Rubinstein)

Our song selection to begin "A New Journey" are:
"Taking Care of Business"...Bachman Turner Overdrive
"Don't Stop Believin'"...Journey
"Here I Go Again"...Whitesnake

Of course, I had to make a trip to Atlanta to see my Grand Babies before I began my new journey. I had a fantastic three days and had tears in my heart when I had to leave.

Keeping the Payers On High Beam
Love and Prayers
Ms. Cathy

8.

Before Cathy had left the hospital, she and Joe met with the bone marrow transplant social worker, who explained how finding a donor process worked. There is an organization named "Be The Match" who has locations all over the world. They travel throughout the country, looking for volunteers that will be willing to have their cheeks swabbed and have their DNA stored in a worldwide data bank. It's much like donating blood to the blood bank, but your DNA does not have an expiration date and to date does not have the use-up rate like blood and platelets. The donors are educated on why they are donating their DNA and having it recorded as well as what the opportunities may present themselves if there was a match found that may need their help.

During their meeting, Cathy learned the following concerning Be The Match organization:

1990 - Nobel Prize in Medicine awarded to Dr. E. Donnall Thomas for discoveries in cellular transplantation

1997 - First use of peripheral blood stem cells in NMDP transplants

1998 - Launched umbilical cord blood transplant program

2001 - Built the NMDP Sample Repository, one of the world's most extensive tissue sample storage facilities used for medical research

2004 - Partnered with the Medical College of Wisconsin to create the Center for International Blood and Marrow Transplant Research® (CIBMTR), our research program

2012 - Completed more than 700 peer-reviewed publications based on research conducted

2013 - Facilitated more than 2,800 transplants for patients over age 50 (45% of total transplants)

2016 - Launched Be The Match BioTherapies® to extend our services and expertise to organizations developing and delivering cellular therapies to help more patients

It did not take Cathy long to realize that not only did she make the correct decision in moving forward with the stem cell transplant, but if her sickness had happened ten years earlier, the chances of her surviving her Leukemia would have significantly been reduced.

During their meeting, Cathy's husband had committed to being her caregiver during the entire process of the transplant. He had been her caregiver since the day she became sick. Still, the responsibilities of the caregiver concerning a stem cell transplant were greater and required some training through webinars and materials provided by Be The Match organization.

After their meeting, they went home and started to digest all of the information that was discussed and what type of preparations needed to be made before they find a donor as well as when the donor is identified and has agreed to the next steps of the process.

The first item on the list was to review the foods that she was not allowed to have vs. the foods that were acceptable. She was not allowed to eat raw vegetables, processed meats or cheeses, or any product from a buffet or cafeteria, any foods that were exposed to open air longer than fifteen to twenty minutes was not to be consumed due to the fear of bacteria. All the vegetables had to be fresh and cleaned before cooking.

All meats had to be prepared well done, and the only fruits she was allowed were fruits that were covered and needed to be peeled before eating, such as bananas and oranges. There were only certain kinds of seafood that were allowed, such as salmon, halibut, cod.

Shrimp, scallops, and clams were not permitted because they were considered bottom feeders. Cathy had three cutting boards, one for red meats, one for chicken, and one for vegetables. Each cutting board had to be scrubbed after each use. Cathy was not permitted to use any condiments or sauce that did not come in its unopened pouch. That meant that she needed her individual packets of mayonnaise, ketchup, mustard, salt, cocktail sauce, relish, syrup, and butter squares. Pepper was not allowed as it tended to contract mold. Joe immediately started the search for how to purchase the above items in bulk quantities. Thanks, Amazon.

The only item that was tough to find was the individually wrapped squares of butter; however, after visiting all of the wholesale clubs in their area, he was able to find one wholesale club that carried the squares in packs of 144. Sam's club was now on his list of good guys that made his mission to take care of his wife a smooth operation. The proactive preparation was going smoothly, and they were ready for that special phone call.

Much to Cathy's surprise, the special phone call came within a few weeks of her going home and restarting her life. The transplant social worker informed her that they had found three potential matches. Two of the matches were international matches, but one was from the United States. The person from the US was her closest match with nine matching numbers, of course, nine was the best you can ask for due to the fact no one knew what Cathy's tenth set of numbers were. Cathy was told that Be The Match was making an effort to contact the person to see if they were still interested in moving forward in donating their stem cells to help a fellow angel.

Everyone at the hospital, as well as Cathy, her husband, along with their three sons, kept their fingers crossed and prayed each day, as they waited for the follow-up phone call informing them of the potential donor's decision. Three days later, the follow-up call came, and Cathy was told that the donor had agreed to move forward with his promise to help someone if there was ever a time in his life that he could. The only information the social worker could share with Cathy at the time was that he was a twenty-year-old male and lives in the state of Pennsylvania. Being that Cathy was born and raised in Pennsylvania, she immediately knew that her prayers were answered.

Cathy and her husband had three days to prepare for her trip to the hospital and begin her new journey to see if she was going to get a second chance of life. There was excitement and happiness that a donor was found, and they agreed to participate in the Be The Match program to help Cathy. But there was also the feeling of concern and fear. Once again, Cathy was blindly journeying into unknown waters in a program that has only been administered for the first time in

1997 and only as recently as 2013, where 2,800 cancer patients over 50 were included in the program. Being that her options were down to only two, she still felt that her decision to participate was the correct one, and the final decision of success or failure was in God's hands, not hers. So once again, she went back to "Keeping the Prayers on High Beam" as she started her trip to the hospital to begin a long and trying year of beating an unrelentless monster named cancer.

Upon arriving at the hospital, they were greeted by their social worker and given a tour of the transplant facility that included the rooms, lounge area, and even a small exercise room. The rooms were very small and compact, with only enough room for a bed and one person other than the patient. When the nurse would come into the room, it was standing room only. The transplant floor area was a completely separate section of the main floor. There was only one way in and out that required you to go through two sets of double doors that could only be opened electronically by a hospital staff member. Each room had its own air filtration system. When they needed to change the air filter, the entire room had to be sealed from the outside. When the new filter was installed, the room would be sealed a second time for three days to allow the system to filter out dust or particles before a patient could be placed in the room.

They discussed patient visiting rules, and her husband was the only person allowed to visit for the time being. The less contact Cathy had with people, the better it would be since her immune system would once again be at an all-time low. Before entering the floor where the rooms were, a person had to get clearance to enter the first set of doors and then wash their hands for forty-five seconds with special liquid soap before being cleared to go through the second set of doors leading to Cathy's room. Cathy and Joe went to her room and prepared it for Cathy's comfort. They then decided to reactivate

Cathy's Corner to bring the support team up to date on what was happening and explain the process of a stem cell transplant. This publication was titled Cathy's Corner "A New Journey Begins," and so the next phase of the battle was in motion, and they would learn soon if it was going to be a positive journey with the ending, they have been working so hard to achieve.

The first course of action was to have a tri-fusion inserted into the left side of Cathy's chest close to the heart. This would serve as the port that would be used to inject the stem cells as well as the anti-rejection drugs and the continuous flow of fluids, after having the Tri-Fusion port surgically inserted into her chest. After a day of rest, Cathy was ready to start the preparation to prepare her body so it could accept her new stem cells without any complications. Her new stem cells were scheduled to be flown to the hospital in a few days. The next phase was another round of chemo that would once again kill all of the cells in her blood, so there was no chance that a lingering cancer cell may be hiding somewhere in her. The chemo treatment went without a problem, and after another day of rest, Cathy was ready for the treatment phase that would prepare her to accept the new stem cells that would be injected into her in a day or so.

However, she was not ready for the severity of the side effects that the serum would cause her body, along with her first feeling of doubt that she had made the right decision. The nurses injected a serum into Cathy that was intended to cleanse her body and prepare her bone marrow to start duplicating the new stem cells. The medical team warned her that the side effects would be harsh, but the procedure was necessary before moving to the phase of stem cell transplant. She had no idea how painful the side effects were going to be. The best way to describe it would be to say that being run over by an eighteen-wheeler truck was like stubbing your toe compared to the deathly sickness you felt from the serum.

For three consecutive days, Cathy felt sick and ached all over; every drink or bite of food came back up immediately. Just the sight or smell of food created a vomiting reaction. Cathy felt that she set a record for the number of times she was heaving her guts out. It was hard to believe it when the nurses told her that her reaction is what they expected, for if she were not having this type of response, it would mean that the serum was not working. The nurse explained to her husband that the serum was derived from the cells and blood from a rabbit. The couple patiently waited for the serum to finish its abusive attack on her body and rejoiced when it was finally over.

The next phase was to wait for the new stem cells to be flown to Orlando from Pennsylvania and driven to the hospital to be administered. On April 1, 2014, a half-gallon-size plastic bag full of stem cells from Pennsylvania was delivered into Cathy's room, and the final steps of preparation began so the stem cells could successfully flow into Cathy's body.

As Joe recorded on his phone the stem cells flowing down the plastic tube into her tri-fusion port, they held hands and prayed that this was going to be the answer that they have waited so patiently for the past ten months. After about one hour, the stem cell bag was empty; Cathy's body had successfully received her new stem cells. The only thing left was the wait to see how her body would react. Would her body accept the new cells and start duplicating them on a continuous replenishment rate 24/7, or would her body reject the stem cells and start destroying them? The next 100 days was going to be the longest 100 days of Cathy's life, and she prayed that her body would accept the new cells, for she was confident that if her body did not, she was not going to go through what she just went through a second time.

Cathy's Corner "A New Journey" 5-6-2014

Hello Everyone. Where did the time go??? I cannot believe it is MAY already!!!!!! I wish I could say time flies when you are having fun, but in my case, that is not true. There has been a lot going on with me, so I guess the best place to start is from the beginning.

I checked into Florida hospital on the 25th of March as scheduled. They started the three days of chemo, which went well. Then the medical team needed to prepare my body for the Stem Cell Transplant. That is when everything started going downhill. They began to give me a three-day regiment of medicines/serums that prepare the bone marrow for the new stem cells; The administering nurse told me that it wasn't chemo; it was worse than chemo.

Well, **that was the biggest understatement since Noah got the weather report of partly cloudy skies.** I was vomiting for four straight days and was so sick I could not believe it. I later learned that the serum was byproducts made from rabbits, and everyone reacts the same way I did.

I thought to myself, Great, this is the rabbit's revenge for the pregnancy tests from the fifties and sixties. So we moved on, and on the 1st of April, I received my new life: a bag of 6 zillion stem cells going into my body. It was pretty cool; you could see these white cells flowing through the tubing and going into my body. I was on my way to being a new person and starting to feel a little better. Everything was moving along, and I was released to go home on the 15th of April (beware of the ides of April). However, my homestay was short. On the 19th of April, I was back in the hospital with a temperature of 101.9.

In the next ten days, I went through multiple tests to see if there was an infection or virus, at which time my feet and legs became very swollen, and I was unable to walk or stand due to the pain. I then went through multiple tests and

Dopplers to make sure there was no blood clot in my legs, lungs, and pelvic area. I later developed GVHD (Graft vs., Host disease), this is a common disease that happens with stem cell transplant, if you are lucky you can get a mild case or if you are unlucky it can be fatal. Right now, they are classifying mine as a little above mild. GVHD is the difference between my cells and my donor's cells and is caused when my donor cells do not recognize my cells and therefore start to attack them, which leaves a bad rash and sores on various parts of your body and are very ugly to view. All I can say is that if they were doing a remake of BEN-HUR, I would be able to qualify as a second in the Leprosy colony scene. I am applying a prescribed crème that is slowing, helping the rash disappear or peel away.

Now back to the infection/virus… I was diagnosed with an active CMV virus. CMV is a virus that is in the body of most people and is dormant and kept in check by your immune system. With all of the meds I was taking to suppress my immune system, my CMV was given a wake-up call and became active.

After a change of a few medicines, I was released to go home on the 28th of April… **Hooray.**

After daily visits to the hospital and having my blood analyzed daily, I was called by my medical nurse on Thursday evening the 1st of May at home. The doctors told me that I needed to return to the hospital on Friday to be readmitted because my CMV had elevated to a level that needed constant monitoring. So that brings me to today and my long-awaited Cathy's Corner update. My medical team is giving me drugs through IV to address the CMV and bring the count down to a more acceptable level. I will probably have a change in Meds that I can take when I go home.

Now that we have all of the challenging days out of the way let's talk about some good news…They did a bone marrow biopsy on Sunday to see how the stem cells are reproducing and see if there is any sign of cancer returning.... Well, the great news is **No cancer.** I am still in complete remission. We are now waiting for the stem cell report, which will show if my bone marrow is reproducing my donor cells or my old cells... SO keep your fingers crossed!!!!!!!!!!!!!!!!!!!!!!!!!!!

Now that brings everyone up to date on what is happening.

Cathy's Comment: If you don't have a few bad days in your life, you will never know the genuine appreciation of your good days.

> *Today's Prayers: please join me in praying for the GVHD to leave, the CMV to fall to a normal count, for my new cells to be my donor cells.*

Today's Songs:
"The Waiting"...Tom Petty and The Heartbreakers
"Mama"...Il Divo—HAPPY MOTHERS DAY

Keeping the Prayers On High Beam
Love and Prayers
Ms. Cathy

9.

In the next few days, Cathy met with her doctors and nurses, and they talked in great detail about the possible side effects, the smorgasbord of drugs that she would be taking, how to live her new normal life when she went home, and clinic follow-up visits. As there were numerous notes to reread and digest, there were two key issues that stood out among the rest. One was that contact with other living humans (except for her caregiver) or animal needed to be kept down to a minimum and, if possible, not at all. Any time she went out of the home, she needed to wear a surgical mask, with no exceptions. The second key issue was to be on the constant alert for GvHD.

Graft-versus-host disease

Medical Complication Graft-versus-host disease is a medical complication following the receipt of transplanted tissue from a genetically different person. GvHD is commonly associated with stem cell transplants, such as those that occur with bone marrow transplants. GVHD also applies to other forms of transplanted tissues, such as solid organ transplants.

Signs of GVHD would be the first signs that a person's body was possibly starting to reject the new stem cells, and the medical team would need to react immediately to try and prevent GVHD from spreading. It was not uncommon for GvHD to show at some time during the first 100 days. However, the severity of its presence could mean that a successful transplant is in jeopardy. Unfortunately, many transplant patients lost their battle as a result of GVHD and not cancer that the transplant was trying to send to the abyss with no return.

After three weeks in the hospital, Cathy was released to come home and recuperate in the comfort of her home. She left the hospital with explicit instructions, which included that if her temperature went up to 100.0 or higher, her caregiver was to call the doctor immediately.

Cathy was so excited to be at home resting and sleeping in her bed. She wore her surgical mask 24/7, even when she was asleep. However, that peace of mind was short-lived, and by the third day, her peace of mind evaporated and was replaced with the fear of losing her fight.

After checking her temperature 100.4 for one hour, it was apparent to her husband that her temperature was not going to show any sign of receding to an average level of 98.6. As instructed, he phoned the doctor and. Left a message, and in three minutes, the doctor had returned his call. They discussed and reviewed the situation over the phone. Without hesitation, the doctor instructed him to bring her to the emergency room, where he would have a medical team waiting for Cathy. Cathy grabbed her bag that had already been packed and sat by the door to the garage just in case she needed to make an unscheduled trip to the hospital.

Once Cathy had been re-admitted to the hospital, the medical team began the process of intravenously starting various fluids, getting blood samples, and calling in the infectious disease team to begin their evaluation of what was happening. Cathy and her husband wanted to believe that this was just a hiccup, and a resolution was close at hand. However, as the tears started flowing down Cathy's face, her husband knew that she was terrified and was fearing the worst.

After two days of treatments, the infectious disease team was able to isolate the problem and began treating the virus that had somehow developed in Cathy. After another two weeks in the hospital, Cathy was once again released to return home and hopefully begin the peace of mind feeling all over again.

Cathy's Corner "A New Journey" 5-24-2014
Hello Support Team..................... Is everyone
ready for a three day weekend?
I know that I am!!!!!!!!!!!!!!!!!!!!!!!!!!!!!!

I finally got out of the hospital last Tuesday evening, and boy was I ready. The medical team worked hard to get all of my numbers in order (White blood cells, Platelets, hemoglobin, and the most important one my CMV). They changed my medicine a few times to try to get a balance of everything I am taking. You know the old story... take this pill for that and take that pill to offset this pill. Right now, I think that I am on about ten types of tablets.

But in spite of everything, I am home, and I am setting a new record of 10 straight days at home. I still have to go to the medical clinic three days a week, where they check my blood, administer fluids, and re-evaluate my meds. It usually takes about 3 - 4 hours to complete the process unless I need blood or platelets, which could make it a long day. I still am not allowed to drive, so my caregiver (Mr. Joe) chauffer's me around to all of my different appointments. Reminds him of his favorite movie, *Driving Miss Daisy*, of course, I am not as irritable as Miss Daisy (most of the time).

It appears that they have the CMV back down to an acceptable level now; we need to keep it there. I still have GVHD (Graft vs. Host Disease) but is also staying in check.

As I stated before, the first 100 days are the most critical, and we are currently on day 52 of 100. Of course, it does not mean that I am healed on day 101, it just means that usually the most severe problems or reactions should happen within the first 100 days. Total healing takes much longer.

NOW THE GOOD NEWS: My doctor told me that the donor cells are 99% in control of my body, which is a person's ultimate goal with Stem Cell transplant. Now I need my body to continue to accept his cells, to start reproducing his cells, and to take his immune system. I guess you can say it is like a caterpillar going through its change, and in the end, it comes out as a beautiful butterfly.

It looks like all of the love and prayers are working. WHAT A GREAT SUPPORT TEAM !!!!!!!!!!!!!!!!!!!!!!!!!

Now we have to be patient, stay positive, and allow the healing to continue its path to a healthy life (and keep all the harmful germs away from me).

Cathy's Comment: In the beginning, I was looking outside myself for strength and confidence, but I quickly learned that it comes from within. It was there all along.

Today's Song Selection goes to the backyard cookout teams.

"Margaretville"...Jimmy Buffet

"Cheeseburger in Paradise"...Jimmy Buffett

"You Never Call me by my Name"...David Allen Cole

A special dedication to Dave and Judy Young for the good times of past Memorial Day weekends we spent together.

I hope everyone has a fun and safe Memorial Day weekend. Joe and I are just staying home and doing the backyard grilling scene and playing Dominoes. But we will have fun, and that is what it is all about.

Keeping the Prayers on High Beam
Love & Prayers
Ms. Cathy

10.

Once Cathy returned home and settled down, it was once again time to restart her new normal lifestyle. Cathy came home with twelve different prescriptions that had to be taken at different times throughout the day. She had anti-rejection drugs, drugs to replenish the minerals she lost as a result of her treatments, medications to counteract the side effects of the anti-rejection drugs, and drugs to counteract the side effects of drugs that were counteracting the side effects of the anti-rejection drugs. Her husband had three alarms set throughout the day so he could keep everything on schedule. Cathy also had to go to the clinic four times a week for treatments and fluids that could last anywhere from six to eight hours each day. After her 100-day quarantine, her visits to the clinic would drop to three days a week and would eventually become less and less over the five years of her transplant care monitoring. When her visits to the clinic went to once a month, she was cleared to drive. The hospital staff loved seeing Cathy; she always brought in cupcakes or some type of treat that she usually baked herself.

Her caregiver was given a break from traveling to the clinic each time. He did not mind the trips to the clinic as he enjoyed the time to relax and read.

Even though it seemed that it took forever, the 100th day of the quarantine had arrived. The medical team did the long-awaited bone marrow test to see how her body was handling her new stem cells. As the doctor was reading the test results to Cathy, tears started flowing down her face; she just could not believe what she was hearing.

The test results showed that her body had accepted her donor's stem cells and was successfully making his DNA. There were no signs of Cathy's old DNA present in her body. She had successfully started her journey to a second chance of life. It was apparent that God had decided that this angel's gift was still needed somewhere in this world. She was not out of the woods yet, but she could see an opening that leads to the fields of flowers and green grass gently swaying in the breeze along with the warmth of the golden sun seeping in.

For the most part, Cathy's continued transplant treatment went without any significant problems or complications. She did get a slight case of GvHD, where her skin was turning different shades of brown. However, this was nothing more than a sign that her body was going through a change. Her doctors gave her a prescription cream that she would rub on the skin where the brown patches would show up. Within a month or so, the brown spots disappeared, and her skin was back to normal.

Cathy had fought a courageous fight, and it appeared that she was winning. No one can say they beat cancer because cancer has many faces, and some of the best hiding places in a person's body. One can merely say they are a cancer survivor, enjoying every day that you remain cancer free.

Thanks to a twenty-year-old stranger from Pennsylvania, Cathy was given a second chance of life. **I guess in the end; you can say that one Angel came forth to help another Angel during a desperate time of need.**

Fairy Tales are more than true, not because they tell us that dragons & monster exists, but because they tell us that dragons and monsters can be beaten. (G.K. Chesterton)

Cathy's Corner – "A New Journey" 7-26-2014
Hello Everyone!!!!!!!! I know it has been a while since our last Cathy's Corner. However, the journey continues, but the hills and valleys are starting to smooth out, and the horizon is looking brighter every week.
I hope everyone is having a great summer so far. Mine has been going well and is improving as the week's pass. The CMV virus is back in line and appears to be staying in the inactive mode right now. I have been hospital free since May 14, and you have no idea how great that feels. The GVHD has run its course, and my skin is back to normal and looking good.

So everything started looking up for me. I am feeling more energetic, getting more energy, and slowly getting my appetite back. It sure was a rough beginning, but I was able to overcome all my challenges get on the right track.

The best part is that I have surpassed my 100 most critical days with no additional setbacks. **NOW THAT IS WORTH A SMALL CELEBRATION.**

THE GOOD NEWS BULLETS: I have been going to the Clinic 3 days a week, where they administer fluids and pull blood and analyze the readings. My blood readings have shown steady improvement, and I am now going two days a week.

My hair is finally starting to grow back, and I am getting eyelashes and eyebrows.

I was able to lose the few extra pounds that the steroids helped me gain.

The medical team performed a bone marrow biopsy after the 1st thirty days of the transplant, and the results showed that my cells are 99% of my donors. Excellent news that shows that we are headed in the right direction.

After 100 days of the most critical days, the medical team performed another bone marrow biopsy. _**Guess What?**_ You got it!!!!! The results showed that my donor cells were still 99% of my cells. In the world of stem cell transplant, 99% is 100%.

Also, the bone marrow showed that I am still cancer free. It is now seven MONTHS OF BEING CANCER FREE!!! NOW THAT IS WHAT I AM TALKING ABOUT!! YEA BABY!!!!!!!!

Food For thought News:

I am still not allowed to drive. I need to be taken off a few of my meds (like the Tacro)

I still don't know what color my hair will be.

My immune system is still suppressed; there are certain uncooked fruits and vegetables that I am still unable to eat.

After I reach my one year mark, I will need to receive all of my vaccinations and immunization shots. Those would be the same ones we received when we were children, i.e., Mumps, smallpox, measles, chickenpox, and so on.

I still cannot eat out, be large crowds, and still need to wear a mask when I am out of the house (even at the clinic).

When you stop and think about everything, you realize that these are small inconveniences that will soon be a distant memory as I move forward in my recovery. I am looking forward to beginning to live my new healthy life.

The stem cell transplant may have started rough, but the end will justify the means. I will grow old, watching my grandchildren grow up to be beautiful young adults. When the time is right, I will share with them stories of my experience and how a team of the best friends ever, along with a special angel, gave me a second chance of life. I will share with them how my friends and angel were always at my side. They never allowed me to fight this battle alone.

Being a cancer survivor is a great accomplishment and one hundred times sweeter when you beat a horrible monster with the help of your family and friends.

As always, I want to thank you for your help, support, and payers you have given me for the past 13 months.

You are the best, and you can hold your head up high with pride and tell people, "I was part of Cathy's Corner winning team."

Today's song selections:
"Feeling Stronger Every Day"...Chicago

"Shout"...The Isley Brothers

"Amazing Grace"...Seven Nations (live)

Until the next Cathy's Corner
Keeping the Prayers on High Beam
Love & Prayers
Ms. Cathy

Cathy's Corner – "A New Journey" Comes to an End, 11-24-2014

Where in the world has this year gone!!!!!! It seems like it was just yesterday I had my stem cell transplant.

They say that when you get older times go faster, I thought with a twenty-year-old's stem cell, it might slow down a little, but apparently not.

I know it has been a while since I have done Cathy's Corner, and I apologize for taking so long, but time has just been flying by.

All in all, I am doing well... very well. I am so excited that the holidays are just right around the corner. Every holiday has a special meaning to me, and I am so thankful for every day and extra grateful for every holiday I can enjoy.

So much has happened since my last update as I continue to progress in my treatment. Below is a brief update on my progress:

I am now going to the clinic once a month... you have no idea how happy the news made me feel. To think that it went from three days a week to two days a week then to 1 day every two weeks and finally to one day a month. I should stay at one day a month until my first anniversary, which is April 1, 2015.

They are still monitoring my blood and doing various blood tests to check and recheck everything. I am currently waiting for my results from my most recent blood draw to see how things are progressing. Keep your fingers crossed.

I no longer need to follow strict food regulations. I am now allowed to eat fresh salads, fruits, and raw vegetables; I don't have to wear a mask when I go out to the store (but I still carry them in my purse, it's flu season), I am allowed to have black pepper, can go out to restaurants to eat. (but I still am not allowed to run the vacuum)

The most important thing to rejoice about is **MY HAIR IS GROWING BACK.** That's is right. I now have a full head of hair not very long but a full head of hair. It is now getting to the point where it will stand up and will not lay flat. (very spikey) but it has grown to the point where I have noticed little wavy spots of hair on my head. They said that my hair could come back different than it was before. It could have taken on some of the characteristics of my donor. The color seems to look a lot like my original color (before the dye), just a little wavy.

The other significant event in my life is that I was able to go back to work part-time. I was working from home and started with four hours. A day and have progressed to six hours—a day. My company has welcomed me back with open arms and many hugs of happiness. It is great to once again be back with people that have been with me in both spirit and prayer since July 2013. It has been a tough journey, but my support team was there with me the whole trip. The kindness and love every one of you has shown me will be in my heart and memories for the rest of my life.

Joe and I had the opportunity to participate in the "Light the Night Walk" for Lymphoma and Leukemia. We were part of the nursing team from Florida Hospital Altamonte Springs. It was an honor to be part of an exceptional group of nurses that shared their gift of healing with me during those eight months of treatment. It was like a reunion of good friends where we laughed and walked to help find a cure for Leukemia. Our team name was "LEUKING FOR A CURE." I hope that I can make this an annual event with my lifelong friends.

Joe and I are looking forward to getting ready for the holidays, and we plan to make a trip to Atlanta between Christmas and the New Year. I can't wait to hold, hug, kiss, and play with grandkids. We still Skype every weekend with our grandchildren, and they both are getting so big.

Beings that I am doing so well getting adjusted to my "new normal lifestyle," I will be making this the final edition of Cathy's Corner "The New Journey." Once again, I want to THANK every one of you for what you have done for these past 18 months. You have no idea how your love, prayers, and support kept me going during those tough days of treatment and recovery. You should all feel very proud of what you did, mostly because you did not have to, but you did it because you genuinely cared and wanted to help.

I will do short and sweet updates from time to time to keep everyone in the loop.

I will end with my song selection, my favorite Cathy's Comments.

MY favorite Cathy's Comments:

Just know, when you truly want success, you will never give up on it. No matter how bad the situation may get.

It is not being without fear, it's having the determination to go on in spite of it. (unknown)

Fairy tales are more than true, not because they tell us that dragons & monster exists, but because they tell us that dragons and monsters can be beaten. (G.K. Chesterton)

I have found that if you love life, life will love you back. (Arthur Rubinstein)

As you know, there many songs that we sang, hummed and played over the past 18 months. Some expressed our feelings, beliefs, and inspired during times of need and somewhere just meant for us to boogey and shake a little booty. I will end with three songs that I feel are appropriate for the day.

"Home Sweet Home"...Motley Crue

"I'm Still Standing"...Elton John

"Can You Feel the Love Tonight"...Elton John

Keeping The Prayers on High Beam (forever)
Love & Prayers
Ms. Cathy

EPILOGUE

Cathy's treatment continued without any significant complications. Some times required her to adjust her lifestyle for a few weeks to get specific blood readings to an acceptable level. Over time her long list of prescriptions dwindled to a few as she continued to make her donors' DNA. A year after the transplant, she was cleared to go back to work, only for part-time to start. Her company welcomed her back with open arms as the majority of them were recipients of Cathy's Corner, and they lived by the slogan "Nobody Fights Alone."

After a year from the transplant date, you are allowed to seek information on the donor. The hospital contacts the social worker who handled the case at the donors' sight, who would then reach out to the donor. However, the donor has the final say and can remain anonymous if they choose to do so. After a month of waiting, Cathy was contacted by her social worker in Florida that the donor did not mind Cathy having contact with him. They began their relationship through e-mails and spent time sharing their history. Cathy learned that his name is Nick, and he lives in a small town in eastern P.A., And he came from a family of three boys. Beings that Cathy has three sons, there was an automatic connection. The highlight of the new friendship came to a climax when Cathy and her husband went to P.A. to meet Nick and his girlfriend in person. They had a four-hour dinner and exchanged an encyclopedia of information. Nick told Cathy that he found Be The Match at his college football game. They had a booth and were educating anyone who wanted to listen about DNA and the worldwide database. All you needed to do was fill out a form and have the person at the booth swab the inside of your cheek. Your DNA would then be stored in the database, and if there were ever a request that you matched someone, Be The Match would contact you to see if you were still interested in participating. Nick stated that he gave blood regularly but thought if he could help change someone's life, he was interested. Nick told Cathy it was almost three years after the swabbing of his cheek that he was contacted about her. He said that he was in the hospital for about three days. They hooked him up to a machine and drew his blood out as it filtered the stem cells from his blood and returned the blood into his body. He was frail following the procedure and needed two days to regain his strength and be released.

In February of 2019, Cathy was released from the Florida Hospital Bone Marrow/Stem Cell transplant center. She was given a clean bill of health and was invited to come back annually for a checkup as long as she continued to bring the cupcakes and cookies that they had grown accustomed to the past five years.

Cathy now has two birthdays, her original September 21 and her new one, April 1. After two years of treatment, a transplant person needs to get all of their immunizations for all of the diseases that they had been previously immune to, such as chickenpox, polio, mumps, measles as well as a few new ones.

She knew that a transplant patient could adapt to the characteristic of the donor, such as the color of eyes, the color of hair, type of hair, skin tone, and even their blood type. Cathy met a transplant patient whose blood type did change to his donors. With that in mind and knowing that Cathy came from a strong German heritage, both her mother and father had an influential German culture. Cathy figured that based on her mother and father, she was somewhere between 88-90% German. Cathy wanted to see if her heritage changed at all, so she did the saliva test through Ancestry.com. When the results came back, she was pleasantly surprised the results showed that she was now 78% Italian with a little German still in there. It was apparent that she was still making Nick's DNA. Joe read the results and started to smile and said, "You know what this means?"

When Cathy answered, "No. What?" He replied, laughing, saying that it means that the Italians are just as bull-headed and stubborn as the Germans. Cathy smiled back and said, "It looks like you didn't come out ahead on the deal." However, after forty-seven years of marriage, her husband felt like he came out alright.

In March of 2019, on Joe's day off, Cathy went back to Florida Hospital and had the port removed that had been embedded in her chest for the past five years. She was now officially cancer free.

Cathy and her husband do not talk much about her two-year battle with an unforgiving, relentless monster. They just look ahead and plan their time together doing fun things, finding reasons to make trips to Atlanta so the can spend time with their grandchildren (they hope that someday, they will be able to move to Georgia so they may be closer to the grandchildren.) They refuse to dwell on the negatives and enjoy the positive ending that was awarded to them.

Cathy and Joe are anxiously waiting to celebrate their 50th wedding anniversary in October 2021. They plan to celebrate their fifty years taking an eight-day Viking River cruise from Amsterdam to Basil, Switzerland.

The only time you should ever look back is to see how far you have come.

Then pause and remember how good life has been

"UNSUNG HEROES"

PROLOGUE

There are medical research teams across America that consist of some of the greatest minds of doctors and scientists in the medical field. These teams are dedicated to finding solutions and treatments that hopefully lead to cures to a variety of sicknesses that plague humankind. One of the most intense researching efforts that have been an ongoing project for many years is the search to find a cure for cancer. Over the years, tremendous progress has been made in developing treatments and medicines that achieve the success of putting cancer in remission. However, finding a cure is still a mystifying challenge since, in most cases, medical science has been unable to identify the origin or source that brings life to this unforgiving monster. At times this monster has the momentum of an out of control wildfire as it rages through one's body, destroying everything in its path.

One of the greatest achievements in modern medicine is the development and use of stem cells and bone marrow transplants as a treatment that can bring success and remission to cancer patients with various types of Leukemia. The development of this procedure has proven to allow Leukemia patients remission and the second chance of a life where ten years ago, their life would have had a different ending. In the early years of trial treatment, the success rate was very low as the trials were using transplants from donors that were a 5, 6, or 7 DNA number match. The recipient's body was just not able to duplicate the DNA with such a low number ratio. As medical science researchers resorted to acquiring a higher DNA set of number matches such as 7, 8, 9, and rare cases 10, the success rate of remission increased and has shown continuous improvement over the past few years. A success rate of 50% to 60% has grown to about 74-76% and continues to show improvement. The success rate is increasing at a slower rate than the medical teams would like. The research teams have stepped up their never-ending testing and development to take the success rate to a new level. They are the tireless workers that have dedicated their lives to make humankind's life better.

During Cathy's stem cell transplant phase of her treatment to send her cancer into remission, she lived and witnessed the highs and lows of a cancer patients fight.

Even though Cathy's fight had a positive outcome, unfortunately, not everyone in her circle of stem cell recipients shared the same positive ending. However, the recipients' loss was not taken lightly. Through conversations with the medical team, it was learned that every piece of information such as, step by step treatment schedules, daily results of the blood test, medicines that were taken and all data from the donor is recorded in a national database and is scrutinized line by line, day by day, drug by drug to see if they can identify where there was a breakdown causing the untimely ending. The medical research team also compares the current data to older data to see if there is some type of pattern or missing piece of the puzzle. The team analyzes and reanalyzes as they retreat, regroup, and develop a plan of reattack for future recipients.

The medical teams across America spend thousands of hours week after week uncompromisingly looking for ways to improve the treatment process and results. Hence, the success rate continues to show improvement.

When you pause and reflect on all of the events that have taken place to bring medical science to where it is today, you realize that there were key players who unknowingly and, in most cases, unwillingly made the ultimate sacrifice that enabled advancements in medicinal practices. These advancements have saved thousands of lives today, giving humanity a second chance of life. We have never met them; we don't know their names, where they lived, felt the warmth of their smiles or touch, felt the love that came from their hearts, or the beauty of their spirit or aura. Still, their ultimate sacrifice and contribution continue to live in the bodies and souls of not only today's survivors but in the hearts of the family's and loved ones. Their sacrifice will help future patients for years to come.

Many will say that they lost their battle to their sickness, but I disagree. They did not lose their battle; they merely ran out time. Those who unwillingly made the ultimate sacrifice are the **_Angels_** that have been called home before our hearts could say goodbye.

**In memory of their ultimate sacrifice, I offer you
"Unsung Heroes"**

What a beautiful morning, the sky was a bright blue with a few cumulus clouds lazily moving across the sun-soaked sky. It was late March, and you could tell that spring was just around the corner. The air felt like Father Winter had finally let go of his grip on the air and was allowing Mother Nature to usher in spring without delay. This past winter was not as cold as in previous years, but the accumulation of snow was above average, and it seemed like the grayness that coated the sky would never leave.

You could not only feel the excitement in the air, but you could see the glow and smiles on everyone's face as they were bustling about doing their long-overdue errands and chores that come with the early days of spring. The hardware stores and nurseries were as busy as bees making honey. Everyone seemed to be on a mission that would bring happiness to their souls.

However, today's warmth and splendor would not be felt by Thomas, for he knew by the end of the day, he would be in a state of remembrance of the fifty-two years he had spent with the love of his life. Thomas was sitting in the hospice room, holding the hand of his wife, Mary Alice, listening as her breathing was becoming more erratic, and she was slowly slipping into an abyss that offered no return.

He had known for some time that this day was not far off. Mary Alice had been fighting a courageous battle with a sickness that was slowly destroying her body, but somehow never affected her spirit. Mary Alice had been battling this sickness for the past five years and was determined never to give up the fight. She always said that when it was over, she would not have lost her battle, but merely ran out of time. She had gone through extensive types of treatment, some in the trial or experimental stage, but to no avail. But she never stopped believing and hoping, for that was how she lived her life.

As Thomas sat there with the love of his life, he began to tell her how much he loved her and what she meant to him and her family. He began to talk about their life together and what a great life it was. Before he realized, he was talking about the first time they met....

As Thomas looked over at the clock radio sitting on the stand next to Mary Alice, he realized that he had been talking for the past six hours about their life together. He also noticed that Mary Alice's breathing was becoming shallower, and he realized that the end was only moments away. He could no longer speak, for he was at a loss for words. What does someone say or do at a time like this? How does someone say a final goodbye? He did not know, for he was never in a position like this before, so he simply bowed his head and said a closing prayer.

Coincidently as he prayed his final word, Mary Alice took her final breath. Her journey on Earth had come to an end, and her new journey began simultaneously. Somehow, Thomas knew it was going to be her best journey yet.

Thomas believed that death is part of living. However, when it happens to the love of your life is the one time that he wished that saying was fictitious. Thomas believed that there must be a meaningful reason and purpose for why Thomas felt the pain he did. Perhaps the pain, sadness, and grief he felt were the final lesson of love that will enable him to create the memories and affection for Mary Alice that will be stored in his heart for the rest of his days.

Thomas stood up and took one final look at his one true love. As the tears started flowing down his face, he gently reached down and kissed her on the forehead and slowly glided down and kissed her on the lips. As he began to stand, he said with a smile on his face, "Thank you, Mary Alice, for enabling me to experience the true meaning of life."

He then turned to find nurse Sandy to tell her that Mary Alice was at peace with this world, but to his surprise, she was already standing at the doorway of the room watching him say his final goodbye. Sandy was deeply saddened because Mary

Alice had touched her heart in her last days at the hospice. Granted, Sandy had experienced death in her years as a nurse, but there was something different about Mary Alice. She had a gift that came from her heart that reached out and touched everyone she encountered. Some people never felt her gift, but those that opened their hearts enjoyed the feeling Mary Alice clairvoyantly conveyed to them without speaking.

As Nurse Sandy looked over to Thomas, she saw the tears streaming down his face, her own heart felt the grief and despair of his loss. She said, "Thomas, I am so sorry for your loss. I know Mary Alice was not only your wife but your best friend as well. I know that she will be deeply missed by everyone whose heart she touched, including mine."

Thomas looked over and said, "Nurse Sandy, you and the medical staff have been nothing but magnificent to both Mary Alice and myself during our stay here. I thank you from the bottom of my heart. However, please do not mistake these tears to be tears of sorrow, for they are 'Tears of Joy.'"

"You see, some things in life are like a two-sided coin. For Mary Alice, one side was our life, and a joyous life for us it was. Together we lived a good life, loving every minute we had. The other side was her sickness. Even though it was a side that brought us hardships and challenges, it was a side that made us stronger as a couple. Because of her sacrifice to try and find a cure for her sickness, progress has been made that can perhaps help someone else from facing the same ending Mary Alice has. So, you see, I am shedding tears of joy from both sides of the coin. Our life together, medical research that may help others, and the fact that Mary Alice is suffering no longer.

"Ms. Sandy, there is an old Native American story that has been passed down over the centuries that was shared when a person's spirit left this world to join the Great Spirit.

. "The chief would call a council and explain to the mourning family that with the loss of a loved one, your heart will be sad and heavy. You will feel two wolves fighting inside of you, each trying to eat the other, one is the wolf of joy, happiness, and love with the other being the wolf of sadness, despair, and grief. When this happens, you must play a part on which wolf will win. When the chief was asked, 'How do I determine which wolf wins?' The chief would stare in their eyes and simply answer, **'it will be the one you feed the most.'**

"So, you see, I am more joyous than I am sad. But I would trade all of my tomorrows for a single yesterday with Mary Alice. But we both know that is not possible, so now all I can do is shed 'Tears of Joy.'"

With his final sentence, Thomas slowly walked out of the hospice room as he took his first steps onto an unknown journey without Mary Alice. As Thomas walked out of the room, Nurse Sandy went over to the side of the bed to pay her final respects to Mary Alice. As she walked to the head of the bed, she saw an unexpected flash of light that lasted a fraction of a second, next she noticed a parchment paper with gold glistens folded under the pillow that Mary Alice's head lay upon. Thinking that Thomas had left something behind, she quickly picked up the paper and looked for Thomas, but he was long gone. She didn't see any writing on the outside of the folded paper, so she began to unfold it to see if it belonged to anyone in particular. To her surprise, it was not addressed to anyone, and it was written in a font that she was not familiar with. It read:

Your medical staff of nurses and doctors have done well with the gift of knowledge I bestowed upon them at birth. They have utilized their gift to continuously improve the well-being of my angels during their brief visit. However, it is now time for me to bring my angel home and heal her spiritually so that she may continue her eternal life.

Sandy just stood there, unable to move a muscle and reread the note for the third time. After a few minutes, she walked over to the window and glanced at the snowcapped mountain that stood a few miles away. As she stood there and watched a golden sunbeam break through the clouds and shine on the top of the mountain, she very quietly whispered, "Thank you for angel Mary Alice. I always knew she was exceptional, and I am honored to have known her.

God speed Mary Alice."

For the first time in more years than Sandy could remember, she felt "Tears of Joy" flowing down her cheeks…

.

Joe's Journal ... Thinking Out Loud

As we begin and continue our journey through life, we quickly discover that life has copious lessons for us. Some of these lessons are simple and easy to understand. However, there are lessons we encounter that are more challenging and difficult to overcome. For the longest time, I felt that the toughest lesson in life would be the loss of a friend or loved one, or in some cases, both. However, in 2013 I realized that losing a loved one who is also your best friend is not the toughest lesson in life. I quickly realized that the toughest lesson in life is to be with a loved one as you witness them, taking the final breath of their life. Fortunately, I was spared that lesson for the time being. However, the possibility that it will always remain to be a reality allows a person to put a higher value on life that many people take for granted. To have a love for life is expected, but to have an undying love for the people in your life is a gift.

I also learned the lesson that if your soulmate develops cancer... **so do you!** You share every step of the journey as you work together to beat an unforgiving monster.

I believe that everyone is born with a gift; some people go through life never realizing or discovering their gift and therefore leave this life with a feeling of an incomplete life. Others do realize their gift, and either use it mistakenly or use it sparingly and never develop it entirely and leave this life with the feeling that they never really hit their potential. Finally, there are the people that realize their gift, embrace it, develop it, and go through life with a feeling of fulfillment. Many times, they utilize their gift unconsciously by merely just being themselves.

I believe that through most of my life, I used my gift unconsciously as I was just me and nothing else. I guess I fit into the cliché' "what you see is what you get." However, Cathy's battle with cancer demanded that I take my gift to heights that I did not realize was possible. During July 2013, I put my clock of life on pause and committed the next two years of my life to be there, helping Cathy wherever and whenever I was needed. There were only two things that mattered in my life: my job and beating an unforgiving monster named cancer. I believe that the real heroes of Cathy's story are the doctors, the medical team, Nick, and of course, Cathy, who fought the most courageous battle of a person's life.

It was amazing to see how everything was orchestrated to an exceptional technique of precise action that sent a monster into an abyss that will hopefully offer no return. Even though my participation was a small part of the equation of success, I would like to think that it was an important piece that provided comfort and peace of mind during the roller coast ride that lasted two years long. The most important thing is the ending was the ending that I always believed would be the way the battle would end. I have no idea why I felt that way, all I know is that if a person believes in something, truly believes with all of their heart without an ounce of doubt, anything is possible.

As I sat back and reflected on all of the events that had occurred in my life, I realized that I had reached the top of my mountain of life. I smiled as I realized that my accomplishments and successes in life outnumbered my disappointments in life by leaps and bounds. I realized that there was nothing more life could offer that will make my heart feel the love and joy that my journey through life has achieved to this point. Anything else would just continue to fill my heart and help it grow to hopefully the size of Texas.

After I completed my self-evaluation, I decided it was time to start my descent down the opposite side of the mountain of life to see what opportunities would present themselves that would allow me to continue to use my gift. So, I began my way down to the bottom, where I can hopefully enjoy the later years of my life. On my descent, I did find various opportunities that allowed me to share the joy and happiness I have stored in my heart as I helped people in a variety of situations.

On my way down the mountain, I did meet a woman who was looking for a person to assist her in providing a service to members of the company she was employed by. She had a gift that allowed her to see somehow and feel my gift in a matter of minutes. After our meeting, she offered me the opportunity to join her in her quest to help the members of the company become "Totally Satisfied" with their involvement as members. I took her up on her offer, and together we worked on helping people become "Totally Satisfied." During my tenure with the company, the final pieces of my puzzle of life fell into place. After another period of self-evaluation, I decided that I still had ambitions in life that I want to achieve before I reached the bottom of my mountain of life. This decision was a difficult one to make considering the enjoyment I received in performing my duties, the comradery of the team I had the pleasure of being part of, and the friendships that were created. However, during my self-evaluation, I realized that in my heart, I felt that I have many tomorrows ahead of me (even though they say tomorrow is never promised to anyone). Still, in reality, my tomorrows are a small percent of the yesterdays that I have already lived.

Therefore, I have once again continued my descend of my mountain of life with tremendous excitement, enthusiasm, and a bucket list of to-dos.

One of my to-dos is to find the answer to the question that has been unanswered for at least 100 years:

"What if the Hokey Pokey **IS** what it is all about."

Life is not waiting for the storm to pass...
It's about learning to dance in the rain.

Vivan Greene

TRUE LOVE
An untold story of love

By Joseph Tristan

We experience love the moment we are born. Love is felt as we are first held and cuddled in our mother's arms continuing the bond that was first created on the day of conception, along with being warmed by the bright smile that is as wide as the Grand Canyon from our Father. Love is the first thing we feel at birth, and love continues to grow not only in us but all around us as we start our journey through life.

Love starts as a simple smile, laugh, hug, warm embrace, soft touch, and perhaps the twinkle in someone's eye. More than likely, the first words we ever heard were, "I Love you."

As we go through life, we encounter many feelings of love, our first ice cream cone, best friends, puppy love, and we can't forget our first kiss; Ahhh!!! Our first kiss, when the seconds seemed to stretch, and you are in this breath that you cannot catch, to finally finding the one **TRUE LOVE** in our life.

Love makes your heart beat a different beat along with a tingling feeling that brings a smile to your face as you ache for that long-lasting effect of feeling the love.

However, as we continue our journey through life and mature as individuals, we learn that love is much more than a heartbeat and tingling feeling. We soon discover that **TRUE LOVE** is like the universe, there is no center, and there is no end. We learn that **TRUE LOVE** is not the feeling you get when the days in life are bright, happy, or pleasant.

TRUE LOVE is the love you feel when the person you love is the person you turn to when you are blue, the person you lean on and cry on their shoulder, the person you share your greatest fears and concerns, the person who stays by your side during your toughest challenges in life and is not only your best friend but the person you believe in.

As we journey through life, we can only hope and pray that the one thing we genuinely accomplish is to experience **TRUE LOVE**.

For, as we experience **TRUE LOVE**, we will have found the true meaning of LIFE.

"CATHY'S CORNER" SONG PLAYLIST

Tile	Artists
Celebration	Kool and the gang.
Devil Went Down to Georgia	Jamison Celtic Rock
The South is Going to do it Again	Charlie Daniels Band
Battleship Chains	Georgia Satellites
The House is a Rocking	Stevie Ray Vaughn
Let It Rock	Georgia Satellites
Pride & Joy	Stevie Ray Vaughn
Dixieland Delight	Alabama
You are My Everything	The Temptations
Get Ready	The Temptations
Dancing in the Streets	Martha Reeves and the Vandellas
Heat Wave	Martha Reeves and the Vandellas
No where to Run	Martha Reeves and the Vandellas
Oh, What a Love	Nitty Gritty Dirt Band
Footstompimg Music	Grand Funk Railroad
Whole Lotts Shakin	Georgia Satellites
Jump, Shout Boogie	Barry Manilow
Home Sweet Home	Motley Crue
All of my rowdy friends are coming over tonight	Hank Williams, Jr.
Strong Enough	Cher
ROLL WITH THE CHANGES	REO SPEEDWAGON
KEEP THE FIRE BURNIN	REO SPEEDWAGON
ANGELS AMONG US	Alabama

IF YOU ARE GOING TO PLAY TEXAS ....Alabama

RAVE ON ....Nitty Gritty Dirt Band

Celebrate Me Home ....Kenny Loggins

Footloose ....Kenny Loggins

Be good to yourself ....Journey

Cherry Bomb ....John Cougar Mellencamp

We're an American Band...Grand Funk Railroad

Twilight Zone ....Golden Earring

Jesus is Just Alright ....The Doobie Brothers

Don't Bring Me Down...E.L.O.

You Have a Friend...James Taylor

Dixie Hoedown ....Nitty Gritty Dirt Band

Gimme Some Lovin' .... Spencer Davis Group

Forever's as far as I'll go ....Alabama

Thank God I'm a Country Boy...John Denver

Free Bird (Live) ....Lynyrd Skynyrd

Orange Blossom Special ....Flying Burrito Brothers

I'll be home for Christmas...Carly Simon

Wizards in Winter...TSO

Mad Russian's Christmas ....TSO

Wish Liszt...TSO

Home for the Holidays...Perry Como

Silent Night ....Susan Boyle

Hark! The Herald Angels Sing...Christmas Joy CD

The Long and Winding Road...The Beatles

Boogie Bumper .... Big Bad Voodoo Daddy

Mambo Swing .... Big Bad Voodoo Daddy

Jumpin Jack .... Big Bad Voodoo Daddy

Gonna Have a Party .... Alabama

Gimme Shelter .... Grand Funk Railroad

How Sweet It Is (To be loved by you) .... James Taylor

I am Women .... Helen Reddy

I won't back down .... Tom Petty

You Light up my Life .... Debbie Boone

You'll Never Walk Alone .... IL Divo

Taking Care of Business .... Bachman Turner Overdrive

Don't Stop Believin' .... Journey

Here I go Again .... Whitesnake

The Waiting .... Tom Petty

Mama .... IL Divo

Margaretville .... Jimmy Buffet

Cheeseburger in paradise .... Jimmy Buffet

You never call me by my name .... David Allen Cole

Feeling Stronger Every Day .... Chicago

Shout .... The Isley Brothers

Amazing Grace .... Seven Nations —Live

Home Sweet Home .... Motley Crue

I'm still standing .... Elton John

Can you feel the love tonight .... Elton John